CW01018815

CURSED
CREATURES

CURSED CREATURES

Edited by Vic Parker

BARDFIELD
PRESS

Contents

Foreword

This book is full of literary creations famous for being fiendish, from Dracula to Frankenstein's monster, along with tales of mummies and vampires, nameless monsters and phantom beasts. Enter a world where dead and buried does not necessarily mean gone forever, and where scraps of corpses and bloodthirsty alter-egos can take on a life of their own.

Ghost stories were popularized during the Victorian era (1837–1901), when families and friends loved nothing more than to gather round the parlour fire on dark evenings to listen to a sinister and spooky story. Spiritualism also became fashionable, and many Victorians dabbled in attempts to contact the dead. Victorian authors transformed Gothic horror-writing, which followed a new and exciting direction. They abandoned remote locations to make their stories more realistic, and in doing so, brought horrors to their readers' front doors.

Vic Parker

The Legend of Sleepy Hollow

Washington Irving

Extract

Several of the Sleepy Hollow people were present at Van Tassel's and, as usual, were doling out their wild and wonderful legends. Many dismal tales were told about funeral trains, and mourning cries and wailings heard and seen about the great tree where the unfortunate Major André was taken, and which stood in the neighbourhood. Some mention was made also of the woman in white, that haunted the dark glen at Raven Rock, and was often heard to shriek on winter nights before a storm, having perished there in the snow. The chief part of the stories, turned upon the favourite spectre of Sleepy Hollow, the Headless Horseman, who had been heard several times of late, patrolling the country; and, it was said, tethered his horse nightly among the graves in the churchyard.

The sequestered situation of this church seems always to have made it a favourite haunt of troubled spirits. It stands on a knoll, surrounded by locust, trees and lofty elms, from among which its decent, whitewashed walls shine modestly forth, like Christian purity beaming through the shades of retirement. A gentle slope descends from it to a silver sheet of water, bordered by high trees, between which, peeps may be caught at the blue hills of the Hudson. To look upon its grass-grown yard, where the sunbeams seem to sleep so quietly, one would think that there at least the dead might rest in peace. On one side of the church extends a wide woody dell, along which raves a large brook among broken rocks and trunks of fallen trees. Over a deep black part of the stream, not far from the church, was formerly thrown a wooden bridge; the road that led to it, and the bridge itself, were thickly shaded by overhanging trees, which cast a gloom about it, even in the daytime; but occasioned a fearful darkness at night. Such was one of the favourite haunts of the Headless Horseman, and the place where he was most frequently encountered. The tale was told of old Brouwer, a most heretical disbeliever in ghosts, how he met the Horseman returning from his foray into Sleepy Hollow, and was obliged to get up behind him; how they galloped over bush and brake, over hill and swamp, until they reached the bridge; when the Horseman suddenly turned into a skeleton, threw old Brouwer into the brook, and sprang away over the treetops with a clap of thunder.

This story was immediately matched by a thrice marvellous adventure of Brom Bones, who made light of the Headless Horseman as an arrant jockey. He affirmed that on returning one night from the neighbouring village of Sing Sing, he had been overtaken by this midnight trooper; that he had offered to race with him for a bowl of punch, and should have won it too, for Daredevil beat the goblin horse all hollow, but just as they came to the church bridge, the Horseman bolted, and vanished in a flash of fire.

All these tales, told in that drowsy undertone with which men talk in the dark, the countenances of the listeners only now and then receiving a casual gleam from the glare of a pipe, sank deep in the mind of Ichabod. He repaid them in kind with large extracts from his invaluable author, Cotton Mather, and added many marvellous events that had taken place in his native state of Connecticut, and fearful sights which he had seen in his nightly walks about Sleepy Hollow.

The revel now gradually broke up. The old farmers gathered together their families in their wagons, and were heard for some time rattling along the hollow roads, and over the distant hills. Some of the damsels mounted on pillions behind their favourite swains, and their lighthearted laughter, mingling with the clatter of hoofs, echoed along the silent woodlands, sounding fainter and fainter, until they gradually died away – and the late scene of noise and frolic was all silent and deserted. Ichabod only lingered behind, according to the custom of country lovers, to have a tête-à-tête with the heiress; fully convinced that he was now on the high road to success. What passed at this interview I will not pretend to say, for in fact I do not know. Something, however, I fear me, must have gone wrong, for he certainly sallied forth, after no very great interval, with an air quite desolate and chopfallen. Oh, these women! These women! Could that girl have been playing off any of her coquettish tricks? Was her encouragement of the poor Ichabod all a mere sham to secure her conquest of his rival? Heaven only knows, not I! Let it suffice to say, Ichabod stole forth with the air of one who had been sacking a hen roost, rather than a fair lady's heart. Without looking to the right or left to notice the scene of rural wealth on which he had so often gloated, he went straight to the stable, and with several hearty cuffs and kicks roused his steed most uncourteously from the comfortable quarters in which he was soundly sleeping, dreaming of mountains of corn and oats, and whole valleys of timothy and clover.

It was the very witching time of night that Ichabod, heavy-hearted and crest fallen, pursued his travels homewards, along the sides of the lofty hills which rise above Tarry Town, and which he had traversed so cheerily in the afternoon. The hour was as dismal as himself. Far below him, the Tappan Zee spread its dusky and indistinct waste of waters, with here and there the tall mast of a sloop, riding quietly at anchor under the land. In the dead hush of midnight, he could even hear the barking of the watchdog from the opposite shore of the Hudson; but it was so vague and faint as only to give an idea of his distance from this faithful companion of man. Now and then, too, the long-drawn crowing of a cock, accidentally awakened, would sound far, far off, from some farmhouse away among the hills – but it was like a dreaming sound in his ear. No signs of life occurred near him, but occasionally the melancholy chirp of a cricket, or perhaps the guttural twang of a bullfrog from a neighbouring marsh, as if sleeping uncomfortably and turning in his bed.

All the stories of ghosts and goblins that he had heard in the afternoon now came crowding upon his recollection. The night grew darker and darker; the stars seemed to sink deeper in the sky, and driving clouds occasionally hid them from his sight. He had never felt so lonely and dismal. He was, moreover, approaching the very place where many of the scenes of the ghost stories had been laid. In the centre of the road stood an enormous tulip tree, which towered like a giant above all the other trees of the neighbourhood, and formed a kind of landmark. Its limbs were gnarled and fantastic, large enough to form trunks for ordinary trees, twisting down almost to the earth and rising again into the air. It was connected with the tragical story of the unfortunate André, who had been taken prisoner hard by; and was universally known by the name of Major André's tree. The common people regarded it with a mixture of respect and superstition, partly out of sympathy for the fate of its ill-starred namesake, and partly from the tales of strange sights, and doleful lamentations told concerning it.

As Ichabod approached this fearful tree, he began to whistle; he thought his whistle was answered – it was but a blast sweeping sharply through the dry branches. As he approached a little nearer, he thought he saw something white hanging in the midst of the tree. He paused, and ceased whistling; but on looking more narrowly, perceived that it was a place where the tree had been scathed by lightning, and the white wood laid bare. Suddenly he heard a groan – his teeth chattered, and his knees smote against the saddle: it was but the rubbing of one huge bough upon another, as they were swayed about by the breeze. He passed the tree in safety, but new perils lay before him.

About two hundred yards from the tree, a small brook crossed the road, and ran into a marshy and thickly wooded glen, known by the name of Wiley's Swamp. A few rough logs, laid side by side, served for a bridge over this stream. On that side of the road where the brook entered the wood, a group of oaks and chestnuts, matted thick with wild grape vines, threw a cavernous gloom over it. To pass this bridge was the severest trial. It was at this identical spot that the unfortunate André was captured, and under the covert of those chestnuts and vines were the sturdy yeomen concealed who surprised him. This has ever since been considered a haunted stream, and fearful are the feelings of the school boy who has to pass it alone after dark.

As he approached the stream his heart began to thump; he summoned up, however, all his resolution, gave his horse half a score of kicks in the ribs, and attempted to dash briskly across the bridge. But instead of starting forward, the perverse old animal made a lateral movement, and ran broadside against the fence. Ichabod, whose fears increased with the delay, jerked the reins on the other side, and kicked lustily with the contrary foot. It was all in vain; his steed started, it is true, but it was only to plunge to the opposite side of the road into a thicket of brambles and alder bushes. The schoolmaster now bestowed both whip and heel upon the starveling ribs of old Gunpowder, who dashed forward, snuffling and snorting, but came to a stand just by the bridge, with a suddenness that had nearly sent his rider sprawling over his head. Just at this moment something by the side of the bridge caught the sensitive ear of Ichabod. In the dark shadow of the grove, on the margin of the brook, he beheld something huge, misshapen and towering. It stirred not, but seemed gathered up in the gloom, like some gigantic monster ready to spring upon the traveller.

The hair of the affrighted schoolmaster rose upon his head

with terror. What was to be done? To turn and fly was now too late; and besides, what chance was there of escaping ghost or goblin, if such it was, which could ride upon the wings of the wind? Summoning up, therefore, a show of courage, he demanded in stammering accents, "Who are you?" He received no reply. He repeated his demand in a still more agitated voice. Still there was no answer. Once more he cudgelled the sides of the inflexible Gunpowder, and, shutting his eyes, broke forth with involuntary fervour into a psalm tune. Just then the shadowy object of alarm put itself in motion, and with a scramble and a bound stood at once in the middle of the road. Though the night was dark and dismal, yet the form of the unknown might now in some degree be ascertained. He appeared to be a horseman of large dimensions, and mounted on a black horse of powerful frame. He made no offer of molestation or sociability, but kept aloof on one side of the road, jogging along on the blind side of old Gunpowder, who had now got over his fright and waywardness.

Ichabod, who had no relish for this strange midnight companion, and bethought himself of the adventure of Brom Bones with the Headless Horseman, now quickened his steed in hopes of leaving him behind. The stranger, however, quickened his horse to an equal pace. Ichabod pulled up, and fell into a walk, thinking to lag behind – the other did the same. His heart began to sink within him; he endeavoured to resume his psalm tune, but his parched tongue clove to the roof of his mouth, and he could not utter a stave. There was something in the moody and dogged silence of this pertinacious companion that was mysterious and appalling. It was soon fearfully accounted for. On mounting a rising ground, which brought the figure of his fellow-traveller in relief against the sky, gigantic in height, and

muffled in a cloak, Ichabod was horror-struck on perceiving that he was headless! But his horror was still more increased on observing that the head, which should have rested on his shoulders, was carried before him on the pommel of the saddle! His terror rose to desperation; he rained a shower of kicks and blows upon Gunpowder, hoping by a sudden movement to give his companion the slip – but the spectre started full jump with him. Away then they dashed, through thick and thin, stones flying and sparks flashing at every bound. Ichabod's flimsy garments fluttered in the air, as he stretched his long lank body away over his horse's head, in the eagerness of his flight.

They had now reached the road which turns off to Sleepy Hollow; but Gunpowder, who seemed possessed with a demon, instead of keeping up it, made an opposite turn, and plunged headlong downhill to the left. This road leads through a sandy hollow shaded by trees for about a quarter of a mile, where it crosses the bridge famous in goblin story, and just beyond swells the green knoll on which stands the whitewashed church.

As yet the panic of the steed had given his unskilful rider an apparent advantage in the chase, but just as he had got halfway through the hollow, the girths of the saddle gave way, and he felt it slipping from under him. He seized it by the pommel, and endeavoured to hold it firm, but in vain; and had just time to save himself by clasping old Gunpowder round the neck, when the saddle fell to the earth, and he heard it trampled underfoot by his pursuer. For a moment the terror of Hans Van Ripper's wrath passed across his mind – for it was his Sunday saddle;

but this was no time for petty fears; the goblin was hard on his haunches, and (unskilful rider that he was!) he had much ado to maintain his seat: sometimes slipping on one side, sometimes another, and sometimes jolted the ridge of his horse's backbone, with a violence that he feared would cleave him asunder.

An opening in the trees now cheered him with the hopes that the church bridge was at hand. The wavering reflection of a silver star in the bosom of the brook told him that he was not mistaken. He saw the walls of the church dimly glaring under the trees beyond. He recollected the place where Brom Bones' ghostly competitor had disappeard. "If I can but reach that bridge," thought Ichabod, " I am safe." Just then he heard the black steed panting and blowing close behind him; he even fancied that he felt his hot breath. Another convulsive kick in

the ribs, and old Gunpowder sprang upon the bridge; he thundered over the resounding planks; he gained the opposite side; and now Ichabod cast a look behind to see if his pursuer should vanish, according to rule, in a flash of fire and brimstone. Just then he saw the goblin rising in his stirrups, and in the very act of hurling his head at him. Ichabod endeavoured to dodge the horrible missile, but too late. It encountered his cranium with a tremendous crash – he was tumbled headlong into the dust, and Gunpowder, the black steed, and the goblin rider, passed by like a whirlwind.

The next morning the old horse was found without his saddle, soberly cropping the grass at his master's gate. Ichabod did not make his appearance at breakfast. Dinner-hour came, but no Ichabod. The boys assembled at the schoolhouse, but no schoolmaster. Hans Van Ripper now began to feel some uneasiness about the fate of poor Ichabod, and his saddle. An inquiry was set on foot, and after diligent investigation they came upon his traces. In one part of the road leading to the church was found the saddle trampled in the dirt; the tracks of horses' hoofs deeply dented in the road, and evidently at furious speed, were traced to the bridge, beyond which, on the bank of a broad part of the brook, where the water ran deep and black, was found the hat of the unfortunate Ichabod, and close beside it a shattered pumpkin.

The brook was searched, but the body of the schoolmaster was not to be discovered.

The Canterville Ghost

Oscar Wilde

Extract

As Canterville Chase is seven miles from Ascot, the nearest railway station, Mr Otis had telegraphed for a waggonette to meet them, and they started on their drive in high spirits. It was a lovely July evening, and the air was delicate with the scent of the pine woods. Now and then they heard a wood pigeon brooding over its own sweet voice, or saw, deep in the rustling fern, the burnished breast of the pheasant. Little squirrels peered at them from the beech trees as they went by, and the rabbits scudded away through the brushwood and over the mossy knolls, with their white tails in the air. As they entered the avenue of Canterville Chase, however, the sky became suddenly overcast with clouds, a curious stillness seemed to hold the atmosphere, a great flight of rooks passed silently over their heads, and, before they reached the house, some big drops of rain had fallen.

Standing on the steps to receive them was an old woman, neatly dressed in black silk, with a white cap and apron. This was Mrs Umney, the housekeeper, whom Mrs Otis, at Lady Canterville's earnest request, had consented to keep on in her former position. She made them each a low curtsey as they alighted, and said in a quaint, old-fashioned manner, "I bid you welcome to Canterville Chase." Following her, they passed through the fine Tudor hall into the library, a long, low room, panelled in black oak, at the end of which was a large stained-glass window. Here they found tea laid out for them, and, after taking off their wraps, they sat down and began to look round, while Mrs Umney waited on them.

Suddenly Mrs Otis caught sight of a dull red stain on the floor just by the fireplace and, quite unconscious of what it really signified, said to Mrs Umney, "I am afraid something has been spilled there."

"Yes, madam," replied the old housekeeper in a low voice, "blood has been spilt on that spot."

"How horrid," cried Mrs Otis. "I don't at all care for bloodstains in a sitting room. It must be removed at once."

The old woman smiled, and answered in the same low, mysterious voice, "It is the blood of Lady Eleanore de Canterville, who was murdered on that very spot by her own husband, Sir Simon de Canterville, in 1575. Sir Simon survived her nine years, and disappeared suddenly under very mysterious circumstances. His body has never been discovered, but his guilty spirit still haunts the Chase. The bloodstain has been much admired by tourists and others, and cannot be removed."

"That is all nonsense," cried Washington Otis. "*Pinkerton's Champion Stain Remover* and *Paragon Detergent* will clean it up in no time," and before the terrified housekeeper could interfere he had fallen upon his knees, and was scouring the floor with a small stick of what looked like a black cosmetic. In a few moments no trace of the bloodstain could be seen.

"I knew *Pinkerton* would do it," he exclaimed triumphantly, as he looked round at his admiring family; but no sooner had he said these words than a terrible flash of lightning lit up the sombre room, a fearful peal of thunder made them all start to their feet, and Mrs Umney fainted.

"What a monstrous climate!" said the American Minister calmly, as he lit a long cheroot. "I guess the old country is so overpopulated that they have not enough decent weather for everybody. I have always been of opinion that emigration is the only thing for England."

"My dear Hiram," cried Mrs Otis, "what can we do with a woman who faints?"

"Charge it to her like breakages," answered the Minister, "she won't faint after that." And in a few moments Mrs Umney certainly came to. There was no doubt, however, that she was extremely upset, and she sternly warned Mr Otis to beware of some trouble coming to the house.

"I have seen things with my own eyes, sir," she said, "that would make any Christian's hair stand on end, and many and many a night I have not closed my eyes in sleep for the awful things that are done here." Mr Otis, however, and his wife warmly assured the honest soul that they were not afraid of ghosts, and, after invoking the blessings of Providence on her new master and mistress, and making arrangements for an increase of salary, the old housekeeper tottered off to her room.

The storm raged fiercely all that night, but nothing of particular note occurred. The next morning, however, when they came down to breakfast, they found the terrible stain of blood once again on the floor. "I don't think it can be the fault of the *Paragon Detergent*," said Washington, "for I have tried it with everything. It must be the ghost." He accordingly rubbed out the stain a second time, but the second morning it appeared again. The third morning also it was there, though the library had been locked up at night by Mr Otis himself, and the key carried upstairs. The whole family were now quite interested; Mr Otis began to suspect that he had been too dogmatic in his denial of the existence of ghosts, Mrs Otis expressed her intention of joining the Psychical Society, and Washington prepared a long letter to Messrs Myers and Podmore on the subject of the permanence of sanguineous stains when connected with crime. That night all doubts about the objective existence of phantasmata were removed forever.

The day had been warm and sunny; and, in the cool of the evening, the whole family went out for a drive. They did not return home till nine o'clock, when they had a light supper. The conversation in no way turned upon ghosts, so there were not even those primary conditions of receptive expectation which so often precede the presentation of psychical phenomena. The subjects discussed, as I have since learned from Mr Otis, were merely such as form the ordinary conversation of cultured Americans of the better class, such as the immense superiority of Miss Fanny Davenport over Sarah Bernhardt as an actress; the difficulty of obtaining green corn, buckwheat cakes, and hominy, even in the best English houses; the importance of Boston in the development of the world-soul; the advantages of the baggage check system in railway travelling; and the sweetness of the New York accent as compared to the London drawl. No mention at all was made of the supernatural, nor was Sir Simon de Canterville alluded to in any way. At eleven o'clock the family retired and by half-past all the lights were out. Some time after, Mr Otis was awakened by a curious noise in the corridor, outside his room. It sounded like the clank of metal, and seemed to be coming nearer every moment. He got up at once, struck a match, and looked at the time. It was exactly one o'clock. He was quite calm, and felt his pulse, which was not at all feverish. The strange noise still continued, and with it he heard distinctly the sound of footsteps. He put on his slippers, took a small oblong phial out of his dressing-case, and opened the door. Right in front of him he saw, in the wan moonlight, an old man of terrible aspect. His eyes were as red as burning coals; long grey hair fell over his shoulders in matted coils; his garments, which were of antique cut, were soiled and ragged, and from his wrists and ankles hung heavy manacles and rusty shackles.

"My dear sir," said Mr Otis, "I really must insist on your oiling those chains, and have brought you for that purpose a small bottle of the *Tammany Rising Sun Lubricator*. It is said to be completely efficacious upon one application, and there are several testimonials to that effect on the wrapper from some of our most eminent native divines. I shall leave it here for you by the bedroom candles, and will be happy to supply you with more should you require it." With these words the United States Minister laid the bottle down on a marble table, and, closing his door, retired to rest.

For a moment the Canterville ghost stood quite motionless in natural indignation; then, dashing the bottle violently upon the polished floor, he fled down the corridor, uttering hollow groans, and emitting a ghastly green light. Just, however, as he reached the top of the great oak staircase, a door was flung open, two little white-robed figures appeared, and a large pillow whizzed past his head! There was evidently no time to be lost, so, hastily adopting the Fourth Dimension of Space as a means of escape, he vanished through the wainscoting, and the house became quite quiet.

On reaching a small secret chamber in the left wing, he leaned up against a moonbeam to recover his breath, and began to try and realize his position. Never, in a brilliant and uninterrupted career of three hundred years, had he been so grossly insulted. He thought of the Dowager Duchess, whom he had frightened into a fit as she stood before the glass in her lace and diamonds; of the four housemaids, who had gone off into hysterics when he merely grinned at them through the curtains of one of the spare bedrooms; of the rector of the parish, whose candle he had blown out as he was coming late one night from the library, and who had been under the care of Sir William Gull ever since, a perfect martyr to nervous disorders; and of old Madame de Tremouillac, who, having wakened up one morning early and seen a skeleton seated in an armchair by the fire reading her diary, had been confined to her bed for six weeks with an attack of brain fever, and, on her recovery, had become reconciled to the Church, and had broken off her connection with that notorious sceptic Monsieur de Voltaire. He remembered the terrible night when the wicked Lord Canterville was found choking in his dressing room, with the knave of diamonds half way down his throat, and confessed, just before he died, that he had cheated Charles James Fox out of £50,000 at Crockford's by means of that very card, and swore that the ghost had made him swallow it. All his great achievements came back to him again, from the butler who had shot himself in the pantry because he had seen a green hand tapping at the window pane, to the beautiful Lady Stutfield, who was always obliged to wear a black velvet band round her throat to hide the mark of five fingers burnt upon her white skin, and who drowned herself at last in the carp-pond at the end of the King's Walk. With the enthusiastic egotism of the true artist he went over his most celebrated performances, and smiled bitterly to himself as he recalled to mind his last appearance as 'Red Ruben, or the Strangled Babe,' his debut as 'Gaunt Gibeon, the Blood-sucker of Bexley Moor,' and the furore he had excited one lovely June evening by merely playing ninepins with his own bones upon the lawn-tennis ground. And after all this, some wretched modern Americans were to come and offer him the *Rising Sun Lubricator*, and throw pillows at his head! It was unbearable. Besides, no ghosts in history had ever been treated in this manner. Accordingly, he determined to have vengeance, and remained till daylight in deep thought.

The next morning when the Otis family met at breakfast, they discussed the ghost at some length. The United States Minister was naturally a little annoyed to find that his present had not been accepted. "I have no wish," he said, "to do the ghost any personal injury, and I must say that, considering the length of time he has been in the house, I don't think it is at all polite to throw pillows at him" – a very just remark, at which, I am sorry to say, the twins burst into shouts of laughter. "Upon the other hand," he continued, "if he really declines to use the

Rising Sun Lubricator, we shall have to take his chains from him. It would be quite impossible to sleep, with such a noise going on outside the bedrooms."

For the rest of the week, however, they were undisturbed, the only thing that excited any attention being the continual renewal of the bloodstain on the library floor. This certainly was very strange, as the door was always locked at night by Mr Otis, and the windows kept closely barred. The chameleon-like colour, also, of the stain excited a good deal of comment. Some mornings it was a dull red, then it would be vermilion, then a rich purple, and once when they came down for family prayers, according to the simple rites of the Free American Reformed Episcopalian Church, they found it a bright emerald-green. These kaleidoscopic changes naturally amused the party very much, and bets on the subject were freely made every evening. The only person who did not enter into the joke was little Virginia, who, for some unexplained reason, was always a good deal distressed at the sight of the bloodstain, and very nearly cried the morning it was emerald-green. The second appearance of the ghost was on Sunday night. Shortly after they had gone to bed they were suddenly alarmed by a fearful crash in the hall. Rushing downstairs, they found that a large suit of old armour had become detached from its stand, and had fallen on the stone floor, while, seated in a high-backed chair, was the Canterville ghost, rubbing his knees with an expression of acute agony on his face. The twins, having brought their peashooters with them, at once discharged two pellets on him, with that accuracy of aim which can only be attained by long and careful practice on a writing-master, while the United States Minister covered him with his revolver, and called upon him, in accordance with Californian etiquette, to hold up his hands! The ghost started up with a wild shriek of rage, and swept through them like a mist, extinguishing Washington Otis's candle as he passed, and so leaving them all in total darkness. On reaching the top of the staircase he recovered himself and determined to give his celebrated peal of demoniac laughter. This he had on more than one occasion found extremely useful. It was said to have turned Lord Raker's wig grey in a single night, and had certainly made three of Lady Canterville's French governesses give warning before their month was up. He accordingly laughed his most horrible laugh, till the old vaulted roof rang and rang again, but hardly had the fearful echo died away when a door opened, and Mrs Otis came out in a light blue dressing gown.

"I am afraid you are far from well," she said, "and have brought you a bottle of *Dr Dobell's Tincture*. If it is indigestion, you will find it a most excellent remedy." The ghost glared at her in fury, and began at once to make preparations for turning himself into a large black dog, an accomplishment for which he was justly renowned, and to which the family doctor always attributed the permanent idiocy of Lord Canterville's uncle, the Hon. Thomas Horton. The sound of approaching footsteps, however, made him hesitate in his fell purpose, so he contented himself with becoming faintly phosphorescent, and vanished with a deep churchyard groan, just as the twins had come up to him.

On reaching his room he entirely broke down, and became a prey to the most violent agitation. The vulgarity of the twins, and the gross materialism of Mrs Otis, were naturally extremely annoying, but what really distressed him most was that he had been unable to wear the suit of mail. He had hoped that even modern Americans would be thrilled by the sight of a Spectre In Armour, if for no more sensible reason, at least out of respect for their national poet Longfellow, over whose graceful and attractive poetry he himself had whiled away many a weary hour when the Cantervilles were up in town. Besides, it was his own suit. He had worn it with success at the Kenilworth tournament, and had been highly complimented on it by no less a person than the Virgin Queen herself. Yet when he had put it on, he had been completely overpowered by the weight of the huge breastplate and steel casque, and had fallen heavily on the stone pavement, barking both his knees severely and bruising the knuckles of his right hand.

For some days after this he was extremely ill, and hardly stirred out of his room at all, except to keep the blood-stain in proper repair. However, by taking great care of himself he recovered, and resolved to make a third attempt to frighten the United States Minister and his family. He a selected Friday the 17th of August for his appearance, and spent most of that day in looking over his wardrobe, ultimately deciding in favour of a large slouched hat with a red feather, a winding-sheet frilled at the wrists and neck, and a rusty sword. Towards evening a violent storm of rain came on, and the wind was so high that all the windows and doors in the old house shook and rattled. In fact, it was just such weather as he loved. His plan of action was this. He was to make his way quietly to Washington Otis's room, gibber at him from the foot of the bed, and stab himself three times in the throat to the sound of slow music. He bore Washington a special grudge, being quite aware that it was he who was in the habit of removing the famous Canterville blood-stain, by means of *Pinkerton's Paragon Detergent*. Having reduced the reckless and foolhardy youth to a condition of abject terror, he was then to proceed to the room occupied by the United States Minister and his wife, and there to place a clammy hand on Mrs Otis's forehead, while he hissed into her trembling husband's ear the awful secrets of the charnel-house. With regard to little Virginia, he had not quite made up his mind. She had never insulted him in any way, and was pretty and gentle. A few hollow groans from the wardrobe, he thought, would be more than sufficient, or, if that failed to wake her, he might grabble at the counterpane with palsy-twitching fingers. As for the twins, he was quite determined to teach them a lesson. The first thing to be done was, of course, to sit upon their chests, so as to produce the stifling sensation of nightmare. Then, as their beds were quite close to each other, to stand between them in the form of a green, icy-cold corpse, till they became paralyzed with fear. And finally, to throw off the winding-sheet and crawl round the room, with white bleached bones and one rolling eyeball, in the character of 'Dumb Daniel, or the Suicide's Skeleton,' a role in which he had on more than one occasion produced a great effect, and which he considered quite equal to his famous part of 'Martin the Maniac, or the Masked Mystery.'

At half past ten he heard the family going to bed. For some time he was disturbed by wild shrieks of laughter from the twins, who, with the lighthearted gaiety of schoolboys, were evidently amusing themselves before they retired to rest, but at a quarter past eleven all was still, and, as midnight sounded, he sallied forth. The owl beat against the window panes, the raven croaked from the old yew tree, and the wind wandered moaning round the house like a lost soul; but the Otis family slept unconscious of their doom, and high above the rain and storm

he could hear the steady snoring of the Minister for the United States. He stepped stealthily out of the wainscoting, with an evil smile on his cruel, wrinkled mouth, and the moon hid her face in a cloud as he stole past the great oriel window, where his own arms and those of his murdered wife were blazoned in azure and gold. On and on he glided, like an evil shadow, the very darkness seeming to loathe him as he passed. Once he thought he heard something call, and stopped; but it was only the baying of a dog from the Red Farm, and he went on, muttering strange sixteenth-century curses, and ever and anon brandishing the rusty sword in the midnight air. Finally he reached the corner of the passage that led to luckless Washington's room. For a moment he paused there, the wind blowing his long grey locks about his head, and twisting into grotesque and fantastic folds the nameless horror of the dead man's shroud. Then the clock struck the quarter, and he felt the time was come. He chuckled to himself and turned the corner; but no sooner had he done so, than, with a piteous wail of terror, he fell back, and hid his blanched face in his long, bony hands. Right in front of him was standing a horrible spectre, motionless as a carven image, and monstrous as a madman's dream! Its head was bald and burnished; its face round, and fat, and white; and hideous laughter seemed to have writhed its features into an eternal grin. From the eyes streamed rays of scarlet light, the mouth was a wide well of fire, and a hideous garment, like to his own, swathed with its silent snows the Titan form. On its breast was a placard with strange writing in antique characters – some scroll of shame it seemed, some record of wild sins, some awful calendar of crime – and, with its right hand, it bore aloft a fashion of gleaming steel.

Never having seen a ghost before, he naturally was terribly frightened and, after a second hasty glance at the awful phantom, he fled back to his room, tripping up in his long winding-sheet as he sped down the corridor, and finally dropping the rusty sword into the Minister's jack boots, where it was found in the morning by the butler. Once in the privacy of his own apartment, he flung himself down on a small pallet-bed and hid his face under the clothes. After a time, however, the brave old Canterville spirit asserted itself and he determined to go and speak to the other ghost as soon as it was daylight. Accordingly, just as the dawn was touching the hills with silver, he returned towards the spot where he had first laid eyes on the grisly phantom, feeling that, after all, two ghosts were better than one, and that, by the aid of his new friend, he might safely grapple with the twins. On reaching the spot, however, a terrible sight met his gaze. Something had evidently happened to the spectre, for the light had entirely faded from its hollow eyes, the gleaming sword had fallen from its hand, and it was leaning up against the wall in a strained and uncomfortable attitude. He rushed forward and seized it in his arms, when, to his horror, the head slipped off and rolled on the floor, the body assumed a recumbent posture, and he found himself clasping a white dimity bed-curtain, with a sweeping-brush, a kitchen cleaver, and a hollow turnip lying at his feet! Unable to understand this curious transformation, he clutched the placard with feverish haste, and there, in the grey morning light, he read these fearful words:

YE OTIS GHOSTE

YE ONLIE TRUE AND ORIGINALE SPOOK
BEWARE OF YE IMITATIONES
ALL OTHERS ARE COUNTERFEITE

The whole thing flashed across him. He had been tricked, foiled, and outwitted! The old Canterville look came into his eyes; he ground his toothless gums together; and, raising his withered hands high above his head, swore, according to the picturesque phraseology of the antique school, that when Chanticleer had sounded twice his merry horn, deeds of blood would be wrought, and Murder walk abroad with silent feet.

Hardly had he finished this awful oath when, from the red-tiled roof of a distant homestead, a cock crew. He laughed a long, low, bitter laugh, and waited. Hour after hour he waited, but the cock, for some strange reason, did not crow again. Finally, at half past seven, the arrival of the housemaids made him give up his fearful vigil, and he stalked back to his room, thinking of his vain hope and baffled purpose. There he consulted several books of ancient chivalry, of which he was exceedingly fond, and found that, on every occasion on which his oath had been used, Chanticleer had always crowed a second time. "Perdition seize the naughty fowl," he muttered, "I have seen the day when, with my stout spear, I would have run him through the gorge, and made him crow for me as 'twere in death!" He then retired to a comfortable lead coffin, and stayed there till evening.

The next day the ghost was very weak and tired. The terrible excitement of the last four weeks was beginning to have its effect. His nerves were completely shattered, and he started at the slightest noise. For five days he kept to his room, and at last made up his mind to give up the point of the bloodstain on the library floor. If the Otis family did not want it, they clearly did not deserve it. They were evidently people on a low, material plane of existence, and quite incapable of appreciating the symbolic value of sensuous phenomena. The question of phantasmic apparitions and the development of astral bodies, was of course quite a different matter, and really not under his control. It was his solemn duty to appear in the corridor once a week, and to gibber from the large oriel window on the first and third Wednesday in every month, and he did not see how he could honourably escape from his obligations. It is quite true that his life had been very evil, but, upon the other hand, he was most conscientious in all things connected with the supernatural. For the next three Saturdays, accordingly, he traversed the corridor as usual between midnight and three o'clock, taking every possible precaution against being either heard or seen. He removed his boots, trod as lightly as possible on the old worm-eaten boards, wore a large black velvet cloak, and was careful to use the *Rising Sun Lubricator* for oiling his chains. I am bound to acknowledge that it was with a good deal of difficulty that he brought himself to adopt this last mode of protection. However, one night, while the family were at dinner, he slipped into Mr Otis's bedroom and carried off the bottle. He felt a little humiliated at first, but afterwards was sensible enough to see that there was a great deal to be said for the invention, and, to a certain degree, it served his purpose. Still, in spite of everything, he was not left unmolested. Strings were continually being stretched across the corridor, over which he tripped in the dark, and on one occasion, while dressed for the part of 'Black Isaac, or the Huntsman of Hogley Woods,' he met with a severe fall, through treading on a butter-slide, which the twins had constructed from the entranccharacter of 'Reckless Rupert, or the Headless Earl.'

He had not appeared in this disguise for more than seventy years; in fact, not since he had so frightened pretty Lady Barbara Modish by means of it, that she suddenly broke off her engagement with the present Lord Canterville's grandfather, and ran away to Gretna Green with handsome Jack Castleton, declaring that nothing in the world would induce her to marry

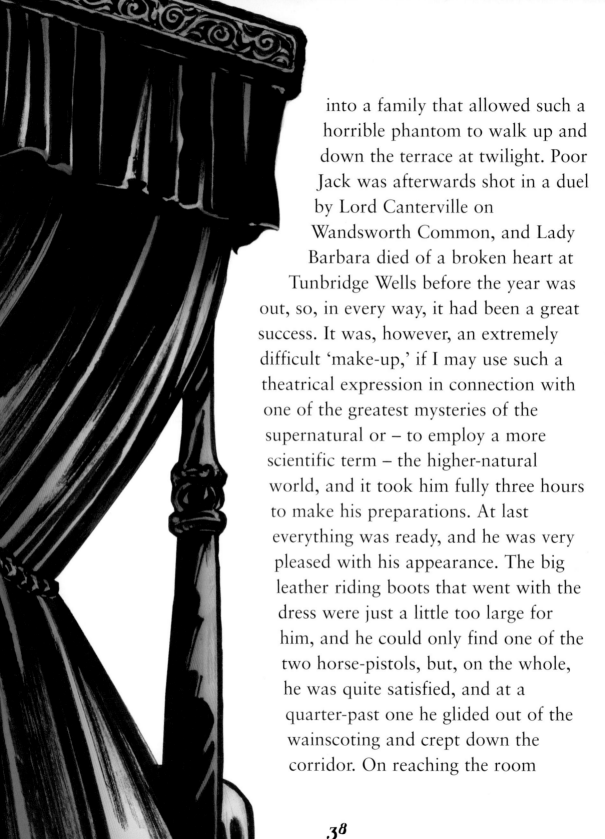

into a family that allowed such a horrible phantom to walk up and down the terrace at twilight. Poor Jack was afterwards shot in a duel by Lord Canterville on Wandsworth Common, and Lady Barbara died of a broken heart at Tunbridge Wells before the year was out, so, in every way, it had been a great success. It was, however, an extremely difficult 'make-up,' if I may use such a theatrical expression in connection with one of the greatest mysteries of the supernatural or – to employ a more scientific term – the higher-natural world, and it took him fully three hours to make his preparations. At last everything was ready, and he was very pleased with his appearance. The big leather riding boots that went with the dress were just a little too large for him, and he could only find one of the two horse-pistols, but, on the whole, he was quite satisfied, and at a quarter-past one he glided out of the wainscoting and crept down the corridor. On reaching the room occupied by the twins, which I should mention was called the Blue Bed Chamber, on account of the colour of its hangings, he found the door just ajar. Wishing to make an effective entrance, he flung it wide open, when a heavy jug of water fell right down on him, wetting him to the skin, and just missing his left shoulder by a couple of inches. At the same moment he heard stifled shrieks of laughter proceeding from the four-poster bed. The shock to his nervous system was so great that he fled back to his room as hard as he could go, and the next day he was laid up with a severe cold. The only thing that at all consoled him in the whole affair was the fact that he had not brought his head with him, for, had he done so, the consequences might have been very serious.

He now gave up all hope of ever frightening this rude, noisy American family, and contented himself as a general rule, with creeping about the passages in list slippers, with a thick red muffler round his throat for fear of draughts, and a small gun, in case he should be attacked by the dreaded twins. The final blow he received occurred on the 19th of September. He had gone downstairs to the great entrance-hall, feeling sure that there, at any rate, he would be quite unmolested, and was amusing himself by making satirical remarks on the large Saroni photographs of the United States Minister and his wife, which had now taken the place of the Canterville family pictures. He was simply but neatly clad in a long shroud, spotted with churchyard mould, and had tied up his jaw with a strip of yellow linen. He carried a small lantern and a sexton's spade. In fact, he was dressed for the character of "Jonas the Graveless, or the Corpse-Snatcher of Chertsey Barn," one of his most remarkable impersonations, and one which the

Cantervilles had every reason to remember, as it was the real origin of their quarrel with their neighbour, Lord Rufford. It was about a quarter-past two o'clock in the morning, and, as far as he could ascertain, no one was stirring. As he was strolling towards the library, however, to see if there were any traces left of the blood-stain, suddenly there leaped out on him from a dark corner two figures, who waved their arms wildly above their heads, and shrieked "BOO!" in his ear.

Seized with a panic, which, under the circumstances, was only natural, he rushed for the staircase, but found Washington Otis waiting for him there with the big garden-syringe; and being thus hemmed in by his enemies on every side, and driven almost to bay, he vanished into the great iron stove, which, fortunately for him, was not lit, and had to make his way home through the flues and chimneys, arriving at his own room in a terrible state of dirt, disorder, and despair.

After this he was not seen again on any nocturnal expedition. The twins lay in wait for him on several occasions, and strewed the passages with nutshells every night to the great annoyance of their parents and the servants, but it was of no avail. It was quite evident that his feelings were so wounded that he would not appear. Mr Otis consequently resumed his great work on the history of the Democratic Party, on which he had been engaged for some years; Mrs Otis organized a wonderful clambake, which amazed the whole county; the boys took to lacrosse, euchre, poker, and other American national games; and Virginia rode about the lanes on her pony, accompanied by the young Duke of Cheshire, who had come to spend the last week of his holidays at Canterville Chase. It was generally assumed that the ghost had gone away, and, in fact, Mr Otis wrote a letter to that effect to Lord Canterville, who, in reply, expressed his great pleasure at the news, and sent his best congratulations to the Minister's wife.

The Otises, however, were deceived, for the ghost was still in the house, and though now almost an invalid, was by no means ready to let matters rest, particularly as he heard that among the guests was the young Duke of Cheshire, whose grand-uncle, Lord Francis Stilton, had once bet a hundred guineas with Colonel Carbury that he would play dice with the Canterville ghost, and was found the next morning lying on the floor of the card room in such a helpless paralytic state, that though he lived on to a great age, he was never able to say anything again but 'Double Sixes.' The story was well known at the time, though, of course, out of respect to the feelings of the two noble families, every attempt was made to hush it up; and a full account of all the circumstances connected with it will be found in the third volume of Lord Tattle's *Recollections of the Prince Regent and his Friends*. The ghost, then, was naturally very anxious to show that he had not lost his influence over the Stiltons, with whom indeed, he was distantly connected, his own first cousin having been married *en secondes noces* to the Sieur de Bulkeley, from whom, as everyone knows, the Dukes of Cheshire are lineally descended. Accordingly, he made arrangements for appearing to Virginia's little lover in his celebrated impersonation of 'The Vampire Monk, or, the Bloodless Benedictine,' a performance so horrible that when old Lady Startup saw it, which she did on one fatal New Year's Eve, in the year 1764, she went off into the most piercing shrieks, which culminated in violent apoplexy, and died in three days, after disinheriting the Cantervilles, who were her nearest relations, and leaving all her money to her London apothecary. At the last moment, however, his terror of the twins prevented his leaving his room, and the little Duke slept in peace under the great feathered canopy in the Royal Bedchamber, and dreamed of Virginia.

Narrative Of a Ghost Of a Hand

J Sheridan Le Fanu

I'm sure she believed every word she related, for old Sally was veracious. But all this was worth just so much as such talk commonly is – marvels, fabulae, what our ancestors called winter's tales – which gathered details from every narrator and dilated in the act of narration. Still it was not quite for nothing that the house was held to be haunted. Under all this smoke there smouldered just a little spark of truth – an authenticated mystery, for the solution of which some of my readers may possibly suggest a theory, though I confess I can't.

Miss Rebecca Chattesworth, in a letter dated late in the autumn of 1753, gives a minute and curious relation of occurrences in the Tiled House, which, it is plain – although at starting she protests against all such fooleries – she has heard with a peculiar sort of interest and relates it certainly with an awful sort of particularity.

I was for printing the entire letter, which is really very singular as well as characteristic. But my publisher meets me with his veto; and I believe he is right. The worthy old lady's letter is, perhaps, too long; and I must rest content with a few hungry notes of its tenor.

That year, and somewhere about the 24th October, there broke out a strange dispute between Mr Alderman Harper, of High Street, Dublin, and my Lord Castlemallard, who, in virtue of his cousinship to the young heir's mother, had undertaken for him the management of the tiny estate on which the Tiled or Tyled House – for I find it spelt both ways – stood.

This Alderman Harper had agreed for a lease of the house for his daughter, who was married to a gentleman named Prosser. He furnished it and put up hangings and otherwise went to considerable expense. Mr and Mrs Prosser came there sometime in June, and after having parted with a good many servants in the interval, she made up her mind that she could not live in the house; and her father waited on Lord Castlemallard and told him plainly that he would not take out the lease because the house was subjected to annoyances which he could not explain. In plain terms, he said it was haunted and that no servants would live there more than a few weeks and that after what his son-in-law's family had suffered there, not only should he be excused from taking a lease of it, but that the

house itself ought to be pulled down as a nuisance and the habitual haunt of something worse than human malefactors.

Lord Castlemallard filed a bill in the Equity side of the Exchequer to compel Mr Alderman Harper to perform his contract, by taking out the lease. But the Alderman drew an answer, supported by no less than seven long affidavits, copies of all which were furnished to his lordship, and with the desired effect; for rather than compel him to place them upon the file of the court, his lordship struck, and consented to release him. I am sorry the cause did not proceed at least far enough to place upon the files of the court the very authentic and unaccountable story which Miss Rebecca relates.

The annoyances described did not begin till the end of August. One evening, Mrs Prosser, quite alone, was sitting in the twilight at the back parlour window. It was open, and looking out into the orchard she plainly saw a hand stealthily placed upon the stone window sill outside, as if by someone beneath the window at her right side, intending to climb up. There was nothing but the hand, which was rather short but handsomely formed and white and plump, laid on the edge of the window sill; and it was not a very young hand, but one aged somewhere about forty, as she conjectured. It was only a few weeks before that the horrible robbery at Clondalkin had taken place and the lady fancied that the hand was that of one of the miscreants who was now about to scale the windows of the Tiled House. She uttered a loud scream and an exclamation of terror and at the same moment the hand was quietly withdrawn.

Search was made in the orchard, but no indications of any person's having been under the window, beneath which, ranged along the wall, stood a great column of flower pots, which it seemed must have prevented anyone's coming within reach of it.

The same night there came a hasty tapping every now and then at the window of the kitchen. The women grew frightened and the servant-man, taking firearms with him, opened the back door, but discovered nothing. As he shut it, however, he said, 'a thump came on it', and a pressure as of somebody striving to force his way in, which frightened him; and though the tapping went on upon the kitchen window panes, he made no further explorations.

About six o'clock on the Saturday evening following, the cook, 'an honest sober woman, now aged nigh sixty years', being alone in the kitchen, saw on looking up, it is supposed, the same fat but aristocratic-looking hand, laid with its palm against the glass, near the side of the window and this time moving slowly up and down, pressed all the while against the glass as if feeling carefully for some inequality in its surface. She cried out and said something like a prayer on seeing it. But it was not withdrawn for several seconds after.

After this, for a great many nights, there came at first a low and afterwards an angry rapping, as it seemed with a set of clenched knuckles, at the back door. And the servant-man would not open it, but called to know who was there; and there came no answer, only a sound as if the palm of the hand was placed against it, and drawn slowly from side to side with a sort of soft, groping motion.

All this time, sitting in the back parlour, which for the time they used as a drawing room, Mr and Mrs Prosser were disturbed by rappings at the window, sometimes very low and furtive, like a clandestine signal, and at others sudden and so loud as to threaten the breaking of the pane.

This was all at the back of the house, which looked upon the orchard as you know. But on a Tuesday night, at about half past nine, there came precisely the same rapping at the hall door; and it went on, to the great annoyance of the master and terror of his wife, at intervals, for nearly two hours.

After this, for several days and nights, they had no annoyance whatsoever and began to think that the nuisance had expended itself. But on the night of the 13th September, Jane Easterbrook, an English maid, having gone into the pantry for the small silver bowl in which her mistress's bedtime drink was served, happening to look up at the little window of only four panes, observed through an augur-hole which was drilled through the window frame for the admission of a bolt to secure the shutter, a white pudgy finger – first the tip and then the two first joints introduced and turned about thus way and that, crooked against the inside, as if in search of a fastening which its owner destined to push aside. When the maid got back into the kitchen, we are told 'she fell into a swounde, and was all the next day very weak.'

Mr Prosser being, I've heard, a hard-headed and conceited

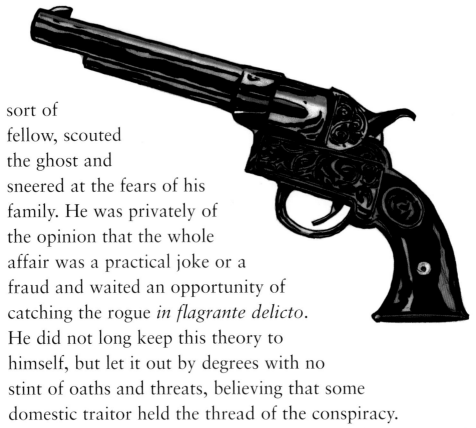

sort of
fellow, scouted
the ghost and
sneered at the fears of his
family. He was privately of
the opinion that the whole
affair was a practical joke or a
fraud and waited an opportunity of
catching the rogue *in flagrante delicto*.
He did not long keep this theory to
himself, but let it out by degrees with no
stint of oaths and threats, believing that some
domestic traitor held the thread of the conspiracy.

Indeed it was time something were done; for not only his
servants, but good Mrs Prosser herself, had grown to look
unhappy and anxious. They kept at home from the hour of
sunset and would not venture about the house after nightfall,
except in couples.

The knocking had ceased for about a week; when one night,
Mrs Prosser being in the nursery, her husband, who was in the
parlour, heard it begin very softly at the hall door. The air was
quite still, which favoured his hearing distinctly. This was the
first time there had been any disturbance at that side of the
house and the character of the summons was changed.

Mr Prosser, leaving the parlour door open it seems, went

quietly into the hall. The sound was that of beating on the outside of the stout door, softly and regularly, 'with the flat of the hand'. He was going to open it suddenly, but changed his mind; and went back very quietly

and on to the head of the kitchen stair, where was a 'strong closet' over the pantry, in which he kept his firearms, swords and canes.

Here he called his manservant, whom he believed to be honest, and with a pair of loaded pistols in his own coat pockets and giving another pair to him, he went as lightly as he could, followed by the man and with a stout walking-cane in his hand, forward to the door.

Everything went as Mr Prosser wished. The besieger of his house, so far from taking fright at their approach, grew more impatient; and the sort of patting which had aroused his attention at first assumed the rhythm and emphasis of a series of double knocks.

Mr Prosser, angry, opened the door with his right arm across, cane in hand. Looking, he saw nothing; but his arm was jerked up oddly, as it might be with the hollow of a hand and something passed under it, with a kind of gentle squeeze. The servant neither saw nor felt anything, and did not know why his master looked back so hastily, cutting with his cane and shutting the door with so sudden a slam.

From that time Mr Prosser discontinued his angry talk and swearing about it and seemed nearly as averse from the subject as the rest of his family. He grew, in fact, very uncomfortable, feeling an inward persuasion that when, in answer to the summons, he had opened the hall door, he had actually given admission to the besieger.

He said nothing to Mrs Prosser, but went up earlier to his bedroom, 'where he read a while in his Bible, and said his prayers'. I hope the particular relation of this circumstance does not indicate its singularity. He lay awake a good while, it appears; and, as he supposed, about a quarter past twelve he heard the soft palm of a hand patting on the outside of the bedroom door and then brushed slowly along it.

Up bounced Mr Prosser, very much frightened, and locked the door, crying, "Who's there?" but receiving no answer, but the same brushing sound of a soft hand drawn over the panels, which he knew only too well.

In the morning the housemaid was terrified by the impression of a hand in the dust of the little parlour table, where they had been unpacking delft and other things the day before. The print of the naked foot in the sea-sand did not frighten Robinson Crusoe half so much. They were by this time all nervous, and some of them half-crazed, about the hand.

Mr Prosser went to examine the mark and made light of it, but, as he swore afterwards, rather to quiet his servants than from any comfortable feeling about it in his own mind. However, he had them all one by one into the room and made each place his or her hand, palm downward, on the same table, thus taking a similar impression from every person in the house, including himself and his wife. And his 'affidavit' deposed that the formation of the hand so impressed differed altogether from those of the living inhabitants of the house and corresponded with that of the hand seen by Mrs Prosser and by the cook.

Whoever or whatever the owner of that hand might be, they all felt his subtle demonstration to mean that it was declared he was no longer out of doors, but had established himself in the house.

And now Mrs Prosser began to be troubled with strange and horrible dreams, some of which as set out in detail, in Aunt Rebecca's long letter, are really very appalling nightmares. But one night, as Mr Prosser closed his bedchamber door, he was struck somewhat by the utter silence of the room, there being no sound of breathing, which seemed strange to him, as he knew his wife was in bed and his ears were particularly sharp.

There was a candle burning on a small table at the foot of the bed, besides the one he held in one hand, a heavy ledger, connected with his father-in-law's business being under his arm. He drew the curtain at the side of the bed and saw Mrs Prosser lying – as for a few seconds he mortally feared – dead, her face being motionless, white, and covered with a cold dew; and on the pillow, close beside her head and just within the curtains, was as he first thought a toad – but really the same fattish hand, the wrist resting on the pillow and the fingers extended towards her temple.

Mr Prosser, with a horrified jerk, pitched the ledger directly at the curtains, behind which the owner of the hand might be supposed to stand. The hand was instantaneously and smoothly snatched away, the curtains made a great wave and Mr Prosser got round the bed in time to see the closet door, which was at the other side, pulled to by the same white, puffy hand, as he believed.

He drew the door open with a fling and stared in: but the closet was empty, except for the clothes hanging from the pegs on the wall and the dressing table and looking-glass facing the windows. He shut it sharply and locked it and felt for a minute, he says, 'as if he were like to lose his wits'. Then, ringing at the bell, he brought the servants and with much ado they recovered Mrs Prosser from a sort of 'trance', in which, he says, from her looks, she seemed to have suffered 'the pains of death': and Aunt Rebecca adds, 'from what she told me of her visions, with her own lips, he might have added, "and of hell also".'

But the occurrence which seems to have determined the crisis was the strange sickness of their eldest child, a little boy aged between two and three years. He lay awake, seemingly in paroxysms of terror, and the doctors who were called in set down the symptoms to incipient water on the brain. Mrs Prosser used to sit up with the nurse by the nursery fire, much troubled in mind about the condition of her child.

His bed was placed sideways along the wall, with its head against the door of a press or cupboard which, however, did not shut quite close. There was a little valance about a foot deep, round the top of the child's bed and this descended within some ten or twelve inches of the pillow on which it lay.

They observed that the little creature was quieter whenever they took it up and held it on their laps. They had just replaced him, as he seemed to have grown quite sleepy and tranquil, but he was not five minutes in his bed when he began to scream in one of his frenzies of terror; at the same moment the nurse for the first time detected, and Mrs Prosser equally plainly saw, following the direction of her eyes, the real cause of the child's sufferings.

Protruding through the aperture of the press and shrouded in the shade of the valance, they plainly saw the white fat hand, palm downwards, presented towards the head of the child. The mother uttered a scream and snatched the child from its little bed, and she and the nurse ran down to the lady's sleeping room, where Mr Prosser was in bed, shutting the door as they entered. They had hardly done so, when a gentle tap came to it from the outside.

There is a great deal more, but this will suffice. The singularity of the narrative seems to me to be this, that it describes the ghost of a hand and no more. The person to whom that hand belonged never once appeared; nor was it a hand separated from a body, but only a hand so manifested and introduced that its owner was always, by some crafty accident, hidden from view.

In the year 1819, at a college breakfast, I met a Mr Prosser – a thin, grave, but rather chatty old gentleman, with very white hair drawn back into a pigtail – and he told us all, with a concise particularity, a story of his cousin, James Prosser, who, when an infant, had slept for some time in what his mother said was a haunted nursery in an old house near Chapelizod and who, whenever he was ill, over-fatigued, or in anywise feverish, suffered all through his life as he had done from a time he could scarce remember, from a vision of a certain gentleman, fat and pale, every curl of whose wig, every button and fold of whose laced clothes and every feature and line of whose sensual, benignant and unwholesome face, was a minutely engraven upon his memory as the dress and lineaments of his own grandfather's portrait, which hung before him every day at breakfast, dinner and supper.

Mr Prosser mentioned this as an instance of a curiously monotonous, individualized and persistent nightmare and hinted the extreme horror and anxiety with which his cousin, of whom he spoke in the past tense as 'poor Jemmie', was at any time induced to mention it.

Narrative of a Ghost of a Hand

I hope the reader will pardon me for loitering so long in the Tiled House, but this sort of lore has always had a charm for me; and people, you know – especially old people – will talk of what most interests themselves, too often forgetting that others may have had more than enough of it.

Wuthering Heights

Emily Brontë
Extract

The business of eating being concluded, I approached a window to examine the weather. A sorrowful sight I saw: dark night coming down prematurely, and sky and hills mingled in one bitter whirl of wind and suffocating snow.

"I don't think it possible for me to get home now without a guide," I could not help exclaiming. "The roads will be buried already. Mrs Heathcliff," I said earnestly, "you must excuse me for troubling you. I presume because, with that face, I'm sure you cannot help being good-hearted. Do point out some landmarks by which I may know my way home"

"Take the road you came," she answered, ensconcing herself in a chair, with a candle and the long book open before her. "It is brief advice, but as sound as I can give."

"Then, if you hear of me being discovered dead in a bog or a pit full of snow, your conscience won't whisper that it is partly your fault?'"

"How so? I cannot escort you. They wouldn't let me go to the end of the garden wall."

"You! I should be sorry to ask you to cross the threshold, for my convenience, on such a night," I cried. "I want you to tell me my way, not to show it: or else to persuade Mr Heathcliff to give me a guide."

"Who? There is himself, Earnshaw, Zillah, Joseph and I."

"Are there no boys at the farm?"

"No; those are all."

"Then, it follows that I am compelled to stay."

"That you may settle with your host. I have nothing to do with it."

"I hope it will be a lesson to you to make no more rash journeys on these hills," cried Heathcliff's stern voice from the kitchen entrance. "As to staying here, I don't keep accommodations for visitors"

"I can sleep on a chair in this room," I replied.

"No, no! A stranger is a stranger, be he rich or poor: it will not suit me to permit anyone the range of the place while I am off guard!" said the unmannerly wretch.

With this insult, my patience was at an end. I uttered an expression of disgust and pushed past him into the yard, running against Earnshaw in my haste. It was so dark that I could not see the means of exit; and, as I wandered round, I heard another specimen of their civil behaviour amongst each other. At first, the young man appeared about to befriend me.

"I'll go with him as far as the park," he said.

"You'll go with him to hell!" exclaimed his master, or whatever relation he bore. "And who is to look after the horses, eh?"

"A man's life is of more consequence than one evening's neglect of the horses; somebody must go," murmured Mrs Heathcliff, more kindly than I expected.

"Not at your command!" retorted Hareton. "If you set store on him, you'd better be quiet."

"Then I hope his ghost will haunt you; and I hope Mr Heathcliff will never get another tenant till the Grange is a ruin," she answered, sharply.

"Hearken, hearken, shoo's cursing on 'em!" muttered Joseph, towards whom I had been steering.

He sat within earshot, milking the cows by the light of a lantern, which I seized unceremoniously and, calling out that I would send it back on the morrow, rushed to the nearest postern.

"Maister, maister, he's staling t' lantern!" shouted the ancient, pursuing my retreat. "Hey, Gnasher! Hey, dog! Hey Wolf, holld him, holld him!"

On opening the little door, two hairy monsters flew at my throat, bearing me down, and extinguishing the light; while a mingled guffaw from Heathcliff and Hareton put the copestone on my rage and humiliation.

Fortunately, the beasts seemed more bent on stretching their paws, and yawning, and flourishing their tails, than devouring me alive; but they would suffer no resurrection, and I was forced to lie till their malignant masters pleased to deliver me. Then, hatless and trembling with wrath, I ordered the miscreants to let me out – on their peril to keep me one minute longer – with several incoherent threats of retaliation that, in their indefinite depth of virulency, smacked of King Lear.

The vehemence of my agitation brought on a copious bleeding at the nose. Still Heathcliff laughed, and still I scolded. I don't know what would have concluded the scene, had there not been one person at hand rather more rational than myself, and more benevolent than my entertainer. This was Zillah, the stout housewife; who at length issued forth to inquire into the nature of the uproar. She thought that some of them had been laying violent hands on me; and, not daring to attack her master, she turned her vocal artillery against the younger scoundrel.

"Well, Mr Earnshaw," she cried, "I wonder what you'll have agait next? Are we going to murder folk on our very door-stones? I see this house will never do for me – look at t' poor lad, he's fair choking! Wisht, wisht; you mun'n't go on so. Come in, and I'll cure that: there now, hold ye still."

With these words she suddenly splashed a pint of icy water down my neck, and pulled me into the kitchen. Mr Heathcliff followed, his accidental merriment expiring quickly.

I was sick exceedingly, and dizzy, and faint; and thus

compelled perforce to accept lodgings under his roof. He told Zillah to give me a glass of brandy, and then passed on to the inner room; while she condoled with me on my sorry predicament, and having obeyed his orders, whereby I was somewhat revived, ushered me to bed.

While leading the way upstairs, she recommended that I should hide the candle, and not make a noise; for her master had an odd notion about the chamber she would put me in, and never let anybody lodge there willingly. I asked the reason. She did not know, she answered: she had only lived there a year or two; and they had so many queer goings on, she could not begin to be curious.

Too stupefied to be curious myself, I fastened my door and glanced round for the bed. The whole furniture consisted of a chair, a clothes press, and a large oak case with squares cut out near the top resembling coach windows. Having approached this structure, I looked inside and perceived it to be a singular sort of old-fashioned couch, very conveniently designed to obviate the necessity for every member of the family having a room to himself. In fact, it formed a little closet, and the ledge of a window, which it enclosed, served as a table. I slid back the panelled sides, pulled them together again, and felt secure against the vigilance of Heathcliff, and everyone else.

The ledge, where I placed my candle, had a few mildewed books piled up in one corner; and it was covered with writing scratched on the wood. This writing, however, was nothing but a name repeated in all kinds of characters, large and small –

'Catherine Earnshaw', here and there varied to 'Catherine Heathcliff', and then again to 'Catherine Linton'.

In vapid listlessness I leant my head against the window, and continued spelling over Catherine Earnshaw – Heathcliff – Linton, till my eyes closed; but they had not rested five minutes when a glare of white letters started from the dark – the air swarmed with Catherines; and rousing myself to dispel the obtrusive name, I discovered my candle-wick reclining on one of the antique volumes, and perfuming the place with an odour of roasted calf-skin. I snuffed it off, and, very ill at ease under the influence of cold and nausea, sat up and spread open the injured tome on my knee. It was a Testament, in lean type, and smelling dreadfully musty: a fly-leaf bore the inscription – 'Catherine Earnshaw, her book,' and a date some quarter of a century back. I shut it, and took up another and another, till I had examined all. Catherine's library was select, and its state of dilapidation proved it to have been well used, though not altogether for a legitimate purpose: scarcely one chapter had escaped a pen-and-ink commentary – at least the appearance of one – covering every morsel of blank that the printer had left. Some were detached sentences; other parts took the form of a regular diary, scrawled in an unformed, childish hand. At the top of an extra page I was greatly amused to behold an excellent caricature of my friend Joseph, – rudely, yet powerfully sketched. An immediate interest kindled within me for the unknown Catherine, and I began forthwith to decipher her faded hieroglyphics.

'An awful Sunday,' commenced the paragraph beneath. 'I wish my father were back again. Hindley is a detestable substitute – his conduct to Heathcliff is atrocious. H and I are going to rebel – we took our initiatory step this evening.

'All day had been flooding with rain; we could not go to church, so Joseph must needs get up a congregation in the garret; and, while Hindley and his wife basked downstairs before a comfortable fire – doing anything but reading their Bibles, I'll answer for it – Heathcliff, myself, and the unhappy ploughboy were commanded to take our prayer books, and mount. We were ranged in a row on a sack of corn, groaning and shivering, and hoping that Joseph would shiver too, so that he might give us a short homily for his own sake. A vain idea! The service lasted precisely three hours; and yet my brother had the face to exclaim, when he saw us descending, "What, done already?" On Sunday evenings we used to be permitted to play, if we did not make much noise; now a mere titter is sufficient to send us into corners.

'"You forget you have a master here," says the tyrant. "I'll demolish the first who puts me out of temper! I insist on perfect sobriety and silence. Oh, boy! was that you? Frances darling, pull his hair as you go by: I heard him snap his fingers." Frances pulled his hair heartily and then went and seated herself on her husband's knee, and there they were, like two babies, kissing and talking nonsense by the hour – foolish palaver that we should be ashamed of. We made ourselves as snug as our means allowed in the arch of the dresser. I had just fastened our pinafores together and hung them up for a curtain, when in comes Joseph, on an errand from the stables. He tears down my handiwork, boxes my ears, and croaks:

'"T' maister nobbut just buried, and Sabbath not o'ered, und t' sound o' t' gospel still i' yer lugs, and ye darr be laiking! Shame on ye! sit ye down, ill childer! There's good books eneugh if ye'll read 'em: sit ye down, and think o' yer sowls!"

'Saying this, he compelled us so to square our positions that we might receive from the far-off fire a dull ray to show us the text of the lumber he thrust upon us. I could not bear the employment. I took my dingy volume by the scroop, and hurled it into the dog kennel, vowing I hated a good book. Heathcliff kicked his to the same place. Then there was a hubbub!

'"Maister Hindley!" shouted our chaplain. " Maister, coom hither! Miss Cathy's riven th' back off 'Th' Helmet o' Salvation,' un' Heathcliff's pawsed his fit into t' first part o' 'T' Brooad Way to Destruction!' It's fair flaysome that ye let 'em go on this gait. Ech! Th' owd man wad ha' laced 'em properly – but he's goan!"

'Hindley hurried up from his paradise on the hearth, and seizing one of us by the collar and the other by the arm, hurled both into the back-kitchen; where, Joseph asseverated, 'owd Nick' would fetch us as sure as we were living: and, so comforted, we each sought a separate nook to await his advent.

'I reached this book, and a pot of ink from a shelf, and pushed the house door ajar to give me light, and I have got the time on with writing for twenty minutes. But my companion is impatient, and proposes that we should appropriate the dairywoman's cloak, and have a scamper on the moors, under its shelter. A pleasant suggestion – and then, if the surly old man come in, he may believe his prophecy verified: we cannot be damper, or colder, in the rain than we are here.'

I suppose Catherine fulfilled her project, for the next sentence took up another subject: she waxed lachrymose.

'How little did I dream that Hindley would ever make me cry so!' she wrote. 'My head aches, till I cannot keep it on the pillow; and still I can't give over. Poor Heathcliff! Hindley calls him a vagabond, and won't let him sit with us, nor eat with us any more; and, he says, he and I must not play together, and threatens to turn him out of the house if we break his orders. He has been blaming our father (how dared he?) for treating H too liberally; and swears he will reduce him to his right place—'

I began to nod drowsily over the dim page: my eye wandered from manuscript to print. I saw a red ornamented title: *Seventy Times Seven, and the First of the Seventy-First. A Pious Discourse delivered by the Reverend Jabez Branderham, in the Chapel of Gimmerden Sough.* And while I was, half consciously, worrying my brain to guess what Jabez Branderham would make of his subject, I sank back in bed, and fell asleep. Alas, for the effects of bad tea and bad temper! What else could it be that made me pass such a terrible night?

I began to dream, almost before I ceased to be sensible of

my locality. I thought it was morning; and I had set out on my way home, with Joseph for a guide. The snow lay yards deep in our road; and, as we floundered on, my companion wearied me with constant reproaches that I had not brought a pilgrim's staff: telling me that I could never get into the house without one, and boastfully flourishing a heavy-headed cudgel, which I understood to be so denominated. For a moment I considered it absurd that I should need such a weapon to gain admittance into my own residence. Then a new idea flashed across me. I was not going there: we were journeying to hear the famous *Jabez Branderham preach, from the text – Seventy Times Seven*; and either Joseph, the preacher, or I had committed the 'First of the Seventy-First,' and were to be publicly exposed and excommunicated.

We came to the chapel. I have passed it really in my walks, twice or thrice; it lies in a hollow, between two hills: an elevated hollow, near a swamp, whose peaty moisture is said to answer all the purposes of embalming on the few corpses deposited there. The roof has been kept whole hitherto; but as the clergyman's stipend is only twenty pounds per annum, and a house with two rooms, threatening speedily to determine into one, no clergyman will undertake the duties of pastor: especially as it is currently reported that his flock would rather let him starve than increase the living by one penny from their own pockets. However, in my dream, Jabez had a full and attentive congregation; and he preached – good God! What a sermon! Divided into *four hundred and ninety* parts, each fully equal to an ordinary address from the pulpit, and each discussing a separate sin! Where he searched for them, I cannot tell. He had his private manner of interpreting the phrase, and it seemed necessary the brother should sin different sins on every occasion.

Oh, how weary I grew. How I writhed, and yawned, and nodded, and revived! How I pinched and pricked myself, and rubbed my eyes, and stood up, and sat down again, and nudged Joseph to inform me if he would ever have done. I was condemned to hear all out: finally, he reached the 'First of the Seventy-First.' At that crisis, a sudden inspiration descended on me; I was moved to rise and denounce Jabez Branderham as the sinner of the sin that no Christian need pardon.

"Sir"' I exclaimed, "sitting here within these four walls, at one stretch, I have endured and forgiven the four hundred and ninety heads of your discourse. Seventy times seven times have I plucked up my hat and been about to depart – seventy times seven times have you preposterously forced me to resume my seat. The four hundred and ninety-first is too much. Fellow-martyrs, have at him! Drag him down, and crush him to atoms, that the place which knows him may know him no more!"

'*Thou art the man!*' cried Jabez, after a pause, leaning over his cushion. "Seventy times seven times didst thou gapingly contort thy visage – seventy times seven did I take counsel with my soul. Lo, this is human weakness: this also may be absolved! The First of the Seventy-First is come. Brethren, execute upon him the judgment written. Such honour have all His saints!"

Wuthering Heights

With that concluding word, the whole assembly, exalting their pilgrim's staves, rushed round me in a body; and I, having no weapon to raise in self-defence, commenced grappling with Joseph, my nearest and most ferocious assailant, for his. In the confluence of the multitude, several clubs crossed; blows, aimed at me, fell on other skulls. Presently the whole chapel resounded with rappings and counter rappings: every man's hand was against his neighbour; and Branderham, unwilling to remain idle, poured forth his zeal in a shower of loud taps on the boards of the pulpit, which responded so smartly that, at last, to my unspeakable relief, they woke me.

And what was it that had suggested the tremendous tumult? What had played Jabez's part in the row? Merely the branch of a fir tree that touched my lattice as the blast wailed by, and rattled its dry cones against the panes! I listened doubtingly an instant; detected the disturber, then turned and dozed, and dreamt again: if possible, still more disagreeably than before.

This time, I remembered I was lying in the oak closet, and I heard distinctly the gusty wind, and the driving of the snow. I heard, also, the fir bough repeat its teasing sound, and ascribed it to the right cause: but it annoyed me so much that I resolved to silence it, if possible; and I thought I rose and endeavoured to unhasp the casement. The hook was soldered into the staple: a circumstance observed by me when awake, but forgotten. "I must stop it, nevertheless!" I muttered, knocking my knuckles through the glass, and stretching an arm out to seize the importunate branch; instead of which, my fingers closed on the fingers of a little, ice-cold hand!

The intense horror of nightmare came over me: I tried to draw back my arm, but the hand clung to it, and a most melancholy voice sobbed, "Let me in – let me in!"

"Who are you?" I asked, struggling, meanwhile, to disengage myself.

"Catherine Linton," it replied, shiveringly (why did I think of Linton? I had read 'Earnshaw' twenty times for Linton).

"I'm come home – I'd lost my way on the moor!"

As it spoke, I discerned, obscurely, a child's face looking through the window. Terror made me cruel; and, finding it useless to attempt shaking the creature off, I pulled its wrist onto the broken pane, and rubbed it to and fro till the blood ran down and soaked the bedclothes. Still it wailed, "Let me in!" and maintained its tenacious gripe, almost maddening me with fear.

"How can I!" I said at length. "Let *me* go, if you want me to let you in!"

The fingers relaxed, I snatched mine through the hole, hurriedly piled the books up in a pyramid against it, and stopped my ears to exclude the lamentable prayer.

I seemed to keep them closed above a quarter of an hour; yet, the instant I listened again, there was the doleful cry moaning on!

"Begone!" I shouted. "I'll never let you in, not if you beg for twenty years."

"It is twenty years," mourned the voice: "twenty years. I've been a waif for twenty years!"

Thereat began a feeble scratching outside, and the pile of books moved as if thrust forward.

I tried to jump up; but could not stir a limb; and so yelled aloud, in a frenzy of fright.

To my confusion, I discovered the yell was not ideal: hasty footsteps approached my chamber door; somebody pushed it open with a vigorous hand, and a light glimmered through the squares at the top of the bed. I sat shuddering yet, and wiping the perspiration from my forehead. The intruder appeared to hesitate, and muttered to himself. At last, he said, in a half-whisper, plainly not expecting an answer, "Is anyone here?"

I considered it best to confess my presence; for I knew Heathcliff's accents, and feared he might search further, if I kept quiet. With this intention, I turned and opened the panels. I shall not soon forget the effect my action produced.

Heathcliff stood near the entrance, in his shirt and trousers; with a candle dripping over his fingers, and his face as white as the wall behind him. The first creak of the oak startled him like an electric shock: the light leapt from his hold to a distance of some feet, and his agitation was so extreme, that he could hardly pick it up.

"It is only your guest, sir," I called out, desirous to spare him the humiliation of exposing his cowardice further. "I had the misfortune to scream in my sleep, owing to a frightful nightmare. I'm sorry I disturbed you."

"Oh, God confound you, Mr Lockwood! I wish you were at the—" commenced my host, setting the candle on a chair, because he found it impossible to hold it steady. "And who showed you up into this room?" he continued, crushing his nails into his palms, and grinding his teeth to subdue the maxillary convulsions. "Who was it? I've a good mind to turn them out of the house this moment!"

"It was your servant, Zillah," I replied, flinging myself onto the floor, and rapidly resuming my garments. "I should not care if you did, Mr Heathcliff; she richly deserves it. I suppose that she wanted to get another proof that the place was haunted, at my expense. Well, it is – swarming with ghosts and goblins! You have reason in shutting it up, I assure you. No one will thank you for a doze in such a den!"

"What do you mean?" asked Heathcliff. "And what are you doing? Lie down and finish out the night, since you *are* here. But, for heaven's sake, don't repeat that horrid noise! Nothing could excuse it, unless you were having your throat cut!"

"If the little fiend had got in at the window, she probably would have strangled me!" I returned. "I'm not going to endure the persecutions of your hospitable ancestors again. Was not the Reverend Jabez Branderham akin to you on the mother's side? And that minx, Catherine Linton, or Earnshaw, or however she was called – she must have been a changeling – wicked little soul! She told me she had been walking the earth these twenty years: a just punishment for her mortal transgressions, I've no doubt!"

Scarcely were these words uttered when I recollected the association of Heathcliff's with Catherine's name in the book, which had completely slipped from my memory, till thus awakened. I blushed at my inconsideration: but, without showing further consciousness of the offence, I hastened to add:

"The truth is, sir, I passed the first part of the night in—" Here I stopped afresh – I was about to say 'perusing those old volumes,' then it would have revealed my knowledge of their written, as well as their printed, contents; so, correcting myself, I went on, "in spelling over the name scratched on that window ledge. A monotonous occupation, calculated to set me asleep, like counting, or—"

"What *can* you mean by talking in this way to *me!*" thundered Heathcliff with savage vehemence. "How – how *dare* you, under my roof? God! He's mad to speak so!" And he struck his forehead with rage.

I did not know whether to resent this language or pursue my explanation; but he seemed so powerfully affected that I took pity and proceeded with my dreams; affirming I had never heard the appellation of 'Catherine Linton' before, but reading it often over produced an impression which personified itself when I had no longer my imagination under control. Heathcliff gradually fell back into the shelter of the bed, as I spoke; finally sitting down almost concealed behind it. I guessed, however, by his irregular and intercepted breathing, that he struggled to vanquish an excess of violent emotion. Not liking to show him that I had heard the conflict, I continued my toilette rather noisily, looked at my watch, and soliloquised on the length of the night: "Not three o'clock yet! I could have taken oath it had been six. Time stagnates here – we must surely have retired to rest at eight!"

"Always at nine in winter, and rise at four," said my host, suppressing a groan and, as I fancied, by the motion of his arm's shadow, dashing a tear from his eyes. "Mr Lockwood," he added, "you may go into my room: you'll only be in the way, coming downstairs so early; and your childish outcry has sent sleep to the devil for me."

"And for me, too," I replied. "I'll walk in the yard till daylight, and then I'll be off; and you need not dread a repetition of my intrusion. I'm now quite cured of seeking pleasure in society, be it country or town. A sensible man ought to find sufficient company in himself."

"Delightful company!" muttered Heathcliff. "Take the candle, and go where you please. I shall join you directly. Keep out of the yard, though, the dogs are unchained; and the house – Juno mounts sentinel there, and – nay, you can only ramble about the steps and passages. But, away with you! I'll come in two minutes!"

I obeyed, so far as to quit the chamber; when, ignorant

where the narrow lobbies led, I stood still, and was witness, involuntarily, to a piece of superstition on the part of my landlord which belied, oddly, his apparent sense. He got onto the bed and wrenched open the lattice, bursting, as he pulled at it, into an uncontrollable passion of tears. "Come in! Come in!" he sobbed. "Cathy, do come. Oh, do – once more! Oh! My heart's darling! Hear me *this* time, Catherine, at last!'

The spectre showed a spectre's ordinary caprice: it gave no sign of being; but the snow and wind whirled wildly through, even reaching my station, and blowing out the light.

There was such anguish in the gush of grief that accompanied this raving, that my compassion made me overlook its folly, and I drew off, half angry to have listened at all, and vexed at having related my ridiculous nightmare, since it produced that agony – though *why* was beyond my comprehension.

I descended cautiously to the lower regions, and landed in the back-kitchen, where a gleam of fire, raked compactly together, enabled me to rekindle my candle. Nothing was stirring except a brindled, grey cat, which crept from the ashes, and saluted me with a querulous mew.

Two benches, shaped in sections of a circle, nearly enclosed the hearth; on one of these I stretched myself, and Grimalkin mounted the other. We were both of us nodding ere anyone invaded our retreat, and then it was Joseph, shuffling down a wooden ladder that vanished in the roof through a trap: the ascent to his garret, I suppose. He cast a sinister look at the little flame which I had enticed to play between the ribs, swept the cat from its elevation, and bestowing himself in the vacancy, commenced the operation of stuffing a three-inch pipe with tobacco. My presence in his sanctum was evidently esteemed a piece of impudence too shameful for remark: he silently applied the tube to his lips, folded his arms, and puffed away. I let him enjoy the luxury unannoyed; and after sucking out his last wreath and heaving a profound sigh, he got up, and departed as solemnly as he came.

A more elastic footstep entered next; and now I opened my mouth for a 'good morning,' but closed it again, the salutation unachieved; for Hareton Earnshaw was chanting *sotto voce*, in a series of curses directed against every object he touched, while he rummaged a corner for a spade or shovel to dig through the drifts. He glanced over the back of the bench, dilating his nostrils, and thought as little of exchanging civilities with me as with my companion the cat. I guessed, by his preparations, that going out was allowed and, leaving my hard couch, made a movement to follow him. He noticed this, and thrust at an inner door with the end of his spade, intimating by an inarticulate sound that there was the place where I must go, if I changed my locality.

It opened into the house, where the females were already astir – Zillah urging flakes of flame up the chimney with a colossal bellows, and Mrs Heathcliff, kneeling on the hearth, reading a book by the aid of the blaze. She held her hand interposed between the furnace heat and her eyes, and seemed absorbed in her occupation; desisting from it only to chide the servant for covering her with sparks, or to push away a dog, now and then, that snoozled its nose overforwardly into her face. I was surprised to see Heathcliff there also. He stood by the fire, his back towards me, just finishing a stormy scene with poor Zillah; who ever and anon interrupted her labour to pluck up the corner of her apron and heave an indignant groan.

"And you, you worthless—" he broke out as I entered, turning to his daughter-in-law, and employing an epithet as harmless as duck, or sheep, but generally represented by a dash. "There you are, at your idle tricks again! The rest of them do earn their bread – you live on my charity! Put your trash away, and find something to do. You shall pay me for the plague of having you eternally in my sight – do you hear, damnable jade?"

"I'll put my trash away, because you can make me if I refuse," answered the young lady, closing her book and throwing it on a chair. "But I'll not do anything, though you should swear your tongue out, except what I please!"

Heathcliff lifted his hand, and the speaker sprang to a safer distance, obviously acquainted with its weight.

Having no desire to be entertained by a cat-and-dog combat, I stepped forward briskly, as if eager to partake the warmth of the hearth, and innocent of any knowledge of the interrupted dispute. Each had enough decorum to suspend further hostilities. Heathcliff placed his fists, out of temptation, in his pockets; Mrs Heathcliff curled her lip and walked to a seat far off, where she kept her word by playing the part of a statue during the remainder of my stay.

The Haunted Dolls' House

M R James

Mr Dillet pointed with his stick to an object which shall be described when the time comes and said: "I suppose you get stuff of that kind through your hands pretty often?" And when he said it, he lied in his throat and knew that he lied. Not once in twenty years – perhaps not once in a lifetime – could Mr Chittenden, skilled as he was in ferreting out the forgotten treasures of half a dozen counties, expect to handle such a specimen. It was a collector's palaver, and Mr Chittenden recognised it as such.

"Stuff of that kind, Mr Dillet! It's a museum piece, that is."

"Well, I suppose there are museums that'll take anything."

"I've seen one, not as good as that, years back," said Mr

Chittenden, thoughtfully. "But that's not likely to come into the market: and I'm told they 'ave some fine ones of the period over the water. No: I'm only telling you the truth, Mr Dillet, when I say that if you was to place an unlimited order with me for the very best that could be got – and you know I 'ave facilities for getting to know of such things and a reputation to maintain – well, all I can say is, I should lead you straight up to that one and say, 'I can't do no better for you than that, sir.'

"Hear, hear!" said Mr Dillet, applauding ironically with the end of his stick on the floor of the shop. "How much are you sticking the innocent American buyer for it, eh?"

"Oh, I shan't be over hard on the buyer, American or otherwise. You see, it stands this way, Mr Dillet – if I knew just a bit more about the pedigree—"

"Or just a bit less," Mr Dillet put in.

"Ha, ha! you will have your joke, sir. No, but as I was saying, if I knew just a little more than what I do about the piece – though anyone can see for themselves it's a genuine thing, every last corner of it, and there's not been one of my men allowed to so much as touch it since it came into the shop – there'd be another figure in the price I'm asking."

"And what's that: five and twenty?"

"Multiply that by three and you've got it, sir. Seventy-five's my price."

"And fifty's mine," said Mr Dillet.

The point of agreement was, of course, somewhere between the two, it does not matter exactly where – I think sixty guineas.

But half an hour later the object was being packed, and within an hour Mr Dillet had called for it in his car and driven away. Mr Chittenden, holding the cheque in his hand, saw him off from the door with smiles and returned, still smiling, into the parlour where his wife was making the tea. He stopped at the door.

"It's gone," he said.

"Thank God for that!" said Mrs Chittenden, putting down the teapot. "Mr Dillet, was it?"

"Yes, it was."

"Well, I'd sooner it was him than another."

"Oh, I don't know, he ain't a bad fellow, my dear."

"Maybe not, but in my opinion he'd be none the worse for a bit of a shake up."

"Well, if that's your opinion, it's my opinion he's put himself into the way of getting one. Anyhow, we shan't have no more of it and that's something to be thankful for."

And so Mr and Mrs Chittenden sat down to tea.

And what of Mr Dillet and of his new acquisition? What it was, the title of this story will have told you. What it was like, I shall have to indicate as well as I can.

There was only just room enough for it in the car and Mr Dillet had to sit with the driver: he had also to go slow, for though the rooms of the Dolls' House had all been stuffed carefully with soft cotton wool, jolting was to be avoided, in view of the immense number of small objects which thronged them; and the ten-mile drive was an anxious time for him, in spite of all the precautions he insisted upon. At last his front door was reached and Collins, the butler, came out.

"Look here, Collins, you must help me with this thing – it's a delicate job. We must get it out upright, see? It's full of little things that mustn't be displaced more than we can help. Let's see, where shall we have it?" He paused, considering. "Really, I think I shall have to put it in my own room, to begin with at any rate. On the big table – that's it."

It was conveyed – with much talking – to Mr Dillet's spacious room on the first floor, looking out on the drive. The sheeting was unwound from it and the front thrown open, and for the next hour or two Mr Dillet was fully occupied in extracting the padding and setting in order the contents of the rooms.

When this thoroughly congenial task was finished, I must say that it would have been difficult to find a more perfect and attractive specimen of a Dolls' House in Strawberry Hill Gothic than that which now stood on Mr Dillet's large kneehole table, lighted up by the evening sun which came slanting through three tall sash-windows.

It was quite six feet long, including the chapel or oratory which flanked the front on the left as you faced it, and the stable on the right. The main block of the house was, as I have said, in the Gothic manner; that is to say, the windows had pointed arches and were surmounted by what are called ogival hoods, with crockets and finials such as we see on the canopies of tombs built into church walls. At the angles were absurd turrets covered with arched panels. The chapel had pinnacles and buttresses and a bell in the turret and coloured glass in the windows. When the front of the house was open you saw four large rooms, bedroom, dining room, drawing room and kitchen, each with its appropriate furniture in a very complete state.

The stable on the right was in two storeys, with its proper complement of horses, coaches and grooms, and with its clock and Gothic cupola for the clock bell.

Pages, of course, might be written on the outfit of the mansion – how many frying pans, how many gilt chairs, what pictures, carpets, chandeliers, four-posters, table linen, glass, crockery and plate it possessed; but all this must be left to the imagination. I will only say that the base or plinth on which the house stood (for it was fitted with one of some depth which allowed of a flight of steps to the front door and a terrace, partly balustraded) contained a shallow drawer or drawers in which were neatly stored sets of embroidered curtains, changes of raiment for the inmates and, in short, all the materials for an infinite series of variations and refittings of the most absorbing and delightful kind.

"Quintessence of Horace Walpole, that's what it is: he must have had something to do with the making of it." Such was Mr Dillet's murmured reflection as he knelt before it in a reverent ecstasy. "Simply wonderful; this is my day and no mistake. Five hundred pound coming in this morning for that cabinet which I never cared about, and now this tumbling into my hands for a tenth, at the very most, of what it would fetch in town. Well, well! It almost makes one afraid something'll happen to counter it. Let's have a look at the population, anyhow."

Accordingly he set them before him in a row. Again, here is an opportunity, which some would snatch at, of making an inventory of costume: I am incapable of it.

There were a gentleman and lady, in blue satin and brocade respectively. There were two children, a boy and a girl. There was a cook, a nurse, a footman and there were the stable servants, two postillions, a coachman, two grooms.

"Anyone else? Yes, possibly."

The curtains of the four-poster in the bedroom were closely drawn round four sides of it and he put his finger in between them and felt in the bed. He drew the finger back hastily, for it almost seemed to him as if something had – not stirred, perhaps, but yielded – in an odd, live way as he pressed it. Then he put back the curtains, which ran on rods in the proper manner, and extracted from the bed a white-haired old gentleman in a long linen nightdress and cap, and laid him down by the rest. The tale was complete.

Dinner time was now near, so Mr Dillet spent but five minutes in putting the lady and children into the drawing room, the gentleman into the dining room, the servants into the kitchen and stables and the old man back into his bed. He retired into his dressing room next door and we see or hear no more of him until something like one o'clock at night.

His whim was to sleep surrounded by some of the gems of his collection. The big room in which we have seen him contained his bed: bath, wardrobe, and all the appliances of dressing were in a commodious room adjoining: but his four-poster, which itself was a valued treasure, stood in the large room where he sometimes wrote and often sat and received visitors. Tonight he repaired to it in a highly complacent frame of mind.

There was no striking clock within earshot – none on the staircase, none in the stable, none in the distant church tower. Yet it is indubitable that Mr Dillet was startled out of a very pleasant slumber by a bell tolling one.

He was so much startled that he did not merely lie breathlessly with wide-open eyes, but actually sat up in his bed.

He never asked himself, till the morning hours, how it was that, though there was no light at all in the room, the Dolls' House on the kneehole table, stood out with complete clearness. But it was so. The effect was that of a bright harvest moon shining full on the front of a big white stone mansion – a quarter of a mile away it might be and yet every detail was photographically sharp. There were trees about it too – trees rising behind the chapel and the house. He seemed to be conscious of the scent of a cool still September night. He thought he could hear an occasional stamp and clink from the stables, as of horses stirring. And with another shock he realized that, above the house, he was looking – not at the wall of his room – but into the profound blue of a night sky.

There were lights, more than one, in the windows, and he quickly saw that this was no four-roomed house with a movable front, but one of many rooms, and staircases – a real house, but seen as if through the wrong end of a telescope. "You mean to show me something," he muttered to himself, and he gazed earnestly on the lighted windows. They would in real life have been shuttered or curtained, no doubt, he thought; but as it was there was nothing to intercept his view of what was being transacted inside the rooms.

Two rooms were lighted – one on the ground floor to the right of the door, one upstairs, on the left – the first brightly enough, the other rather dimly. The lower room was the dining room: a table was laid, but the meal was over and only wine and glasses were left on the table. The man of the blue satin and the woman of the brocade were alone in the room and they were talking very earnestly, seated close together at the table, their elbows on it: every now and again stopping to listen, as it seemed. Once *he* rose, came to the window and opened it and put his head out and his hand to his ear. There was a lighted taper in a silver candlestick on a sideboard. When the man left the window he seemed to leave the room also; and the lady, taper in hand, remained standing and listening. The expression on her face was that of one striving her utmost to keep down a fear that threatened to master her – and succeeding. It was a hateful face, too; broad, flat and sly. Now the man came back and she took some small thing from him and hurried out of the room. He too, disappeared, but only for a moment or two. The front door slowly opened and he stepped out and stood on the top of the *perron*, looking this way and that; then turned towards the upper window that was lighted and shook his fist.

It was time to look at that upper window. Through it was seen a four-poster bed: a nurse or other servant in an armchair, evidently sound asleep; in the bed an old man lying: awake and, one would say, anxious, from the way in which he shifted about and moved his fingers, beating tunes on the coverlet. Beyond the bed a door opened. Light was seen on the ceiling and the lady came in: she set down her candle on a table, came to the fireside and roused the nurse. In her hand she had an old-fashioned wine bottle, ready uncorked. The nurse took it, poured some of the contents into a little silver saucepan, added some spice and sugar from casters on the table and set it to warm on the fire. Meanwhile the old man in the bed beckoned feebly to the lady, who came to him, smiling, took his wrist as if to feel his pulse and bit her lip as if in consternation. He looked at her anxiously and then pointed to the window and spoke. She nodded and did as the man below had done; opened the casement and listened – perhaps rather ostentatiously; then drew her head in and shook it, looking at the old man, who seemed to sigh.

By this time the posset on the fire was steaming and the nurse poured it into a small two-handled silver bowl and brought it to the bedside. The old man seemed disinclined for it and was waving it away, but the lady and the nurse together bent over him and evidently pressed it upon him. He must have yielded, for they supported him into a sitting position and put it to his lips. He drank most of it, in several draughts, and they laid him down. The lady left the room, smiling goodnight to him, and took the bowl, the bottle and the silver saucepan with her. The nurse returned to the chair and there was an interval of complete quiet.

Suddenly the old man started up in his bed – and he must have uttered some cry, for the nurse started out of her chair and made but one step of it to the bedside. He was a sad and terrible sight –– flushed in the face, almost to blackness, the eyes glaring whitely, both hands clutching at his heart, foam at his lips.

For a moment the nurse left him, ran to the door, flung it wide open, and one supposes, screamed aloud for help, then darted

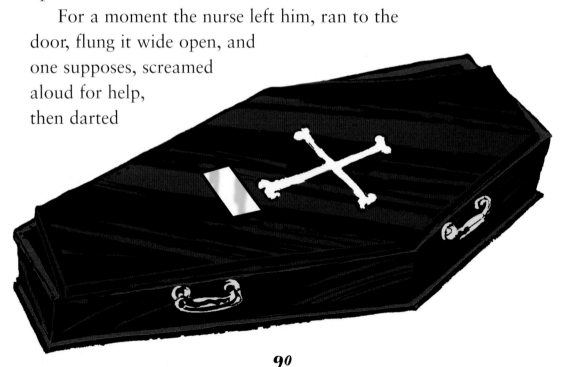

back to the bed and seemed to try feverishly to soothe him – to lay him down – anything. But as the lady, her husband and several servants, rushed into the room with horrified faces, the old man collapsed under the nurse's hands and lay back and the features, contorted with agony and rage, relaxed slowly into calm.

A few moments later, lights showed out to the left of the house and a coach with flambeaux drove up to the door. A white-wigged man in black got nimbly out and ran up the steps, carrying a small leather trunk-shaped box. He was met in the doorway by the man and his wife, she with her handkerchief clutched between her hands, he with a tragic face, but retaining his self-control. They led the newcomer into the dining room, where he set his box of papers on the table and, turning to them, listened with a face of consternation at what they had to tell. He nodded his head again and again, threw out his hands slightly, declined, it seemed, offers of refreshment and lodging for the night and within a few minutes came slowly down the steps, entering the coach and driving off the way he had come. As the man in blue watched him from the top of the steps, a smile not pleasant to see stole slowly over his fat white face. Darkness fell over the whole scene as the lights of the coach disappeared.

But Mr Dillet remained sitting up in the bed: he had rightly guessed that there would be a sequel. The house front glimmered out again before long. But now there was a difference. The lights were in other windows, one at the top of the house, the other illuminating the range of coloured windows of the chapel. How he saw through these is not quite obvious, but he did. The interior was as carefully furnished as the rest of the establishment, with its minute red cushions on the desks, its Gothic stall-canopies and its western gallery and pinnacled organ with gold pipes. On the centre of the black and white pavement was a bier: four tall candles burned at the corners. On the bier was a coffin covered with a pall of black velvet.

As he looked the folds of the pall stirred. It seemed to rise at one end: it slid downwards: it fell away, exposing the black coffin with its silver handles and nameplate. One of the tall candlesticks swayed and toppled over. Ask no more, but turn, as Mr Dillet hastily did, and look in at the lighted window at the top of the house, where a boy and girl lay in two truckle-beds, and a four-poster for the nurse rose above them. The nurse was not visible for the moment; but the father and mother were there, now in mourning, but with very little sign of mourning in their demeanour. Indeed, they were laughing and talking with a good deal of animation, sometimes to each other and sometimes throwing a remark to one or other of the children and again laughing at the answers. Then the father was seen to go on tiptoe out of the room, taking with him as he went a white garment that hung on a peg near the door. He shut the door after him. A minute or two later it was slowly opened again and a muffled head poked round it. A bent form of sinister shape stepped across to the truckle-beds and suddenly stopped, threw up its arms and revealed, of course, the father, laughing. The children were in agonies of terror, the boy with the bedclothes over his head, the girl throwing herself out of bed into her mother's arms. Attempts at consolation followed – the parents took the children on their laps, patted them, picked up the white gown and showed there was no harm in it and so forth; and at last putting the children back into bed, left the room with encouraging waves of the hand. As they lcft it, the nurse came in and soon the light died down. Still Mr Dillet watched immovable.

A new sort of light – not of lamp or candle – a pale ugly light, began to dawn around the door-case at the back of the room. The door was opening again. The seer does not like to dwell upon what he saw entering the room: he says it might be described as a frog – the size of a man – but it had scanty white hair about its head. It was busy about the truckle-beds, but not for long. The sound of cries – faint, as if coming out of a vast distance – but even so, infinitely appalling, reached the ear. There were signs of a hideous commotion all over the house: lights passed along and up, and doors opened and shut, and running figures passed within the windows. The clock in the stable turret tolled one and darkness fell again.

It was only dispelled once more, to show the house front. At the bottom of the steps dark figures were drawn up in two lines, holding flaming torches. More dark figures came down the steps, bearing, first one, then another small coffin. And the lines of torch-bearers with the coffins between them moved silently onward to the left.

The hours of night passed on – never so slowly, Mr Dillet thought. Gradually he sank down from sitting to lying in his bed – but he did not close an eye: and early next morning he sent for the doctor.

The doctor found him in a disquieting state of nerves and recommended sea air. To a quiet place on the east coast he accordingly repaired by easy stages in his car.

One of the first people he met on the sea front was Mr Chittenden, who, it appeared, had likewise been advised to take his wife away for a bit of a change.

Mr Chittenden looked somewhat askance upon him when they met: and not without cause.

"Well, I don't wonder at you being a bit upset, Mr Dillet. What? Yes, well, I might say 'orrible upset, to be sure, seeing what me and my poor wife went through ourselves. But I put it to you, Mr Dillet, one of two things: was I going to scrap a lovely piece like that on the one 'and, or was I going to tell customers: 'I'm selling you a regular picture-palace-drama in real life of the olden time, billed to perform regular at one o'clock a.m.'? Why, what would you 'ave said yourself? And next thing you know, two Justices of the Peace in the back parlour and pore Mr and Mrs Chittenden off in a spring cart to the County Asylum and everyone in the street saying, 'Ah, I thought it 'ud come to that. Look at the way the man drank!' – and me next door, or next door but one, to a total abstainer, as you know. Well, there was my position. What? Me 'ave it back in the shop? Well, what do *you* think? No, but I'll tell you what I will do. You shall have your money back, bar the ten pound I paid for it, and you make what you can."

Later in the day, in what is offensively called the 'smoke room' of the hotel, a murmured conversation between the two went on for some time.

"How much do you really know about that thing and where it came from?"

"Honest, Mr Dillet, I don't know the 'ouse. Of course, it came out of the lumber room of a country 'ouse – that anyone could guess. But I'll go as far as say this, that I believe it's not a hundred miles from this place. Which direction and how far I've no notion. I'm only judging by guesswork. The man as I actually paid the cheque to ain't one of my regular men and I've lost sight of him; but I 'ave the idea that this part of the country was his beat and that's every word I can tell you. But now, Mr Dillet, there's one thing that rather physics me. That old chap – I suppose you saw him drive up to the door – I thought so: now, would he have been the medical man, do you take it? My wife would have it so, but I stuck to it that was the lawyer, because he had papers with him and one he took out was folded up."

"I agree," said Mr Dillet. "Thinking it over, I came to the conclusion that was the old man's will, ready to be signed."

"Just what I thought," said Mr Chittenden, "and I took it that will would have cut out the young people, eh? Well, well! It's been a lesson to me, I know that. I shan't buy no more dolls' houses, nor waste no more money on the pictures – and as to this business of poisonin' grandpa, well, if I know myself, I never 'ad much of a turn for that. Live and let live: that's bin my motto throughout life and I ain't found it a bad one, that's for sure."

Filled with these elevated sentiments, Mr Chittenden retired to his lodgings. Mr Dillet next day repaired to the local Institute, where he hoped to find some clue to the riddle that absorbed him. He gazed in despair at a long file of the Canterbury and York Society's publications of the Parish Registers of the district. No print resembling the house of his nightmare was among those that hung on the staircase and in the passages. Disconsolate, he found himself in a derelict room, staring at a dusty model of a church in a dark and dusty glass case:

"Model of St Stephen's Church, Coxham. Presented by J. Merewether, Esq., of Ilbridge House, 1877. The work of his ancestor James Merewether, d. 1786."

There was something in the fashion of it that reminded him dimly of his horror. He retraced his steps to a wall map he had noticed, and made out that Ilbridge House was in Coxham Parish. Coxham was, as it happened, one of the parishes of which he had retained the name when he glanced over the file of printed registers and it was not long before he found in them the record of the burial of Roger Milford, aged 76, on the 11th September 1757, and of Roger and Elizabeth Merewether, aged nine and seven, on the 19th of the same month. It seemed worthwhile to follow up this clue, frail as it was; and in the afternoon he drove out to Coxham. The east end of the north aisle of the church is a Milford chapel and on its north wall are tablets to the same persons; Roger, the elder, it seems, was distinguished by all the qualities which adorn 'the Father, the Magistrate, and the Man': the memorial was erected by his attached daughter Elizabeth, 'who did not long survive the loss of a parent ever solicitous for her welfare, and of two amiable children'. The last sentence was plainly an addition to the original inscription.

A yet later slab told of James Merewether, husband of Elizabeth, 'who in the dawn of life practised, not without success, those arts which, had he continued their exercise, might in the opinion of the most competent judges have earned for him the name of the British Vitruvius: but who, overwhelmed by the visitation which deprived him of an affectionate partner and a blooming offspring, passed his Prime and Age in a secluded yet elegant Retirement: his grateful Nephew and Heir indulges a pious sorrow by this too brief recital of his excellences'.

The children were more simply commemorated. Both died on the night of the 12th of September.

Mr Dillet felt sure that in Ilbridge House he had found the scene of his drama. In some old sketch book, possibly even in some old print, he may yet find some convincing evidence that he is right. But the Ilbridge House of today is not that which he sought; it is an Elizabethan erection of the forties, in mellow red brick, with stone quoins and dressings. A quarter of a mile from it, in a low part of the park, backed by ancient, stag-horned, ivy-strangled trees and thick undergrowth, are marks of a terraced platform overgrown with rough, dry grass. A few stone balusters lie here and there, and a heap or two, covered with nettles, brambles and ivy, of wrought stones with badly carved crockets. This, someone told Mr Dillet, was the site of a much

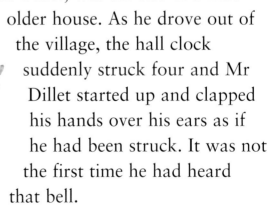

older house. As he drove out of the village, the hall clock suddenly struck four and Mr Dillet started up and clapped his hands over his ears as if he had been struck. It was not the first time he had heard that bell.

98

The Haunted Dolls' House

Awaiting an offer from the other side of the Atlantic, the dolls' house still reposes, carefully sheeted, in a loft over Mr Dillet's stables, whither Collins conveyed it on the day when Mr Dillet started for the sea coast.

A Christmas Carol

Charles Dickens
Extract

Scrooge took his melancholy dinner in his usual melancholy tavern; and having read all the newspapers, and beguiled the rest of the evening with his banker's-book, went home to bed. He lived in chambers which had once belonged to his deceased partner. They were a gloomy suite of rooms, in a lowering pile of building up a yard, where it had so little business to be, that one could scarcely help fancying it must have run there when it was a young house, playing at hide-and-seek with other houses, and have forgotten the way out again. It was old enough now, and dreary enough, for nobody lived in it but Scrooge, the other rooms being all let out as offices. The yard was so dark that even Scrooge, who knew its every stone, was fain to grope with his hands. The fog and frost so hung about the black old gateway of the house, that it seemed as if the Genius of the Weather sat in mournful meditation on the threshold.

Now, it is a fact, that there was nothing at all particular about the knocker on the door, except that it was very large. It is also a fact, that Scrooge had seen it, night and morning, during his whole residence in that place; also that Scrooge had as little of what is called fancy about him as any man in the City of London, even including – which is a bold word – the corporation, aldermen, and livery. Let it also be borne in mind that Scrooge had not bestowed one thought on Marley, since his last mention of his seven-years dead partner that afternoon. And then let any man explain to me, if he can, how it happened that Scrooge, having his key in the lock of the door, saw in the knocker, without its undergoing any intermediate process of change: not a knocker, but Marley's face.

Marley's face. It was not in impenetrable shadow as the other

objects in the yard were, but had a dismal light about it, like a bad lobster in a dark cellar. It was not angry or ferocious, but looked at Scrooge as Marley used to look:
with ghostly spectacles turned up upon its ghostly forehead. The hair was curiously stirred, as if by breath or hot air; and, though the eyes were wide open, they were perfectly motionless. That, and its livid colour, made it horrible; but its horror seemed to be in spite of the face and beyond its control, rather than a part of its own expression.

As Scrooge looked fixedly at this phenomenon, it was a knocker again. To say that he was not startled, or that his blood was not conscious of a terrible sensation to which it had been a stranger from infancy, would be untrue. But he put his hand upon the key he had relinquished, turned it sturdily, walked in, and lighted his candle.

He *did* pause, with a moment's irresolution, before he shut the door; and he *did* look cautiously behind it first, as if he half expected to be terrified with the sight of Marley's pigtail sticking out into the hall. But there was nothing on the back of the door, except the screws and nuts that held the knocker on, so he said "Pooh, pooh!" and closed it with a bang.

The sound resounded through the house like thunder. Every room above, and every cask in the wine-merchant's cellars below, appeared to have a separate peal of echoes of its own. Scrooge was not a man to be frightened by echoes. He fastened the door, and walked across the hall, and up the stairs, slowly too: trimming his candle as he went.

You may talk vaguely about driving a coach-and-six up a good old flight of stairs; but I mean to say you might have got a hearse up that staircase, and taken it broadwise, with the splinter-bar towards the wall and the door towards the balustrades: and done it easy. There was plenty of width for that, and room to spare; which is perhaps the reason why Scrooge thought he saw a locomotive hearse going on before him in the gloom. Half-a-dozen gas lamps out of the street wouldn't have lighted the entry too well, so you may suppose that it was pretty dark with Scrooge's dip.

Up Scrooge went, not caring a button for that: darkness is cheap, and Scrooge liked it. But before he shut his heavy door, he walked through his rooms to see that all was right. He had just enough recollection of the face to desire to do that.

Sitting room, bedroom, lumber room. All as they should be. Nobody under the table, nobody under the sofa; a small fire in the grate; spoon and basin ready; and the little saucepan of gruel (Scrooge had a cold in his head) upon the hob. Nobody under the bed; nobody in the closet; nobody in his dressing gown, which was hanging up in a suspicious attitude against the wall. Lumber room as usual. Old fire guard, old shoes, two fish-baskets, wash-stand on three legs, and a poker.

Quite satisfied, he closed his door, and locked himself in; double locked himself in, which was not his custom. Thus secured against surprise, he took off his cravat; put on his dressing gown and slippers, and his night cap; and sat down before the fire to take his gruel.

It was a very low fire indeed; nothing on such a bitter night. He was obliged to sit close to it, and brood over it, before he could extract the least sensation of warmth from such a handful of fuel. The fireplace was an old one, built by some Dutch merchant long ago, and paved all round with quaint Dutch tiles, designed to illustrate the Scriptures. There were Cains and Abels, Pharaoh's daughters, Queens of Sheba, Angelic messengers descending through the air on clouds like feather-beds, Abrahams, Belshazzars, Apostles putting off to sea in butter-boats, hundreds of figures to attract his thoughts; and yet that face of Marley, seven years dead, came like the ancient Prophet's rod, and swallowed up the whole. If each smooth tile had been a blank at first, with power to shape some picture on its surface from the disjointed fragments of his thoughts, there would have been a copy of old Marley's head on every one.

"Humbug!" said Scrooge; and walked across the room.

After several turns, he sat down again. As he threw his head back in the chair, his glance happened to rest upon a bell, a disused bell, that hung in the room, and communicated for some purpose now forgotten with a chamber in the highest storey of the building. It was with great astonishment, and with a strange, inexplicable dread, that as he looked, he saw this bell begin to swing. It swung so softly in the outset that it scarcely made a sound; but soon it rang out loudly, and so did every bell in the house.

This might have lasted half a minute, or a minute, but it seemed an hour. The bells ceased as they had begun, together.

They were succeeded by a clanking noise, deep down below; as if some person were dragging a heavy chain over the casks in the wine-merchant's cellar. Scrooge then remembered to have heard that ghosts in haunted houses were described as dragging chains.

The cellar door flew open with a booming sound, and then he heard the noise much louder, on the floors below; then coming up the stairs; then coming straight towards his door.

"It's humbug still!" said Scrooge. "I won't believe it."

His colour changed though, when, without a pause, it came on through the heavy door, and passed into the room before his eyes. Upon its coming in, the dying flame leaped up, as though it cried, "I know him! Marley's Ghost!" and fell again.

The same face: the very same. Marley in his pigtail, usual waistcoat, tights and boots; the tassels on the latter bristling, like his pigtail, and his coat-skirts, and the hair upon his head. The chain he drew was clasped about his middle. It was long, and wound about him like a tail; and it was made (for Scrooge observed it closely) of cash boxes, keys, padlocks, ledgers, deeds, and heavy purses wrought in steel. His body was transparent; so that Scrooge, observing him, and looking through his waistcoat, could see the two buttons on his coat behind.

Scrooge had often heard it said that Marley had no bowels, but he had never believed it until now.

No, nor did he believe it even now. Though he looked the phantom through and through, and saw it standing before him;

though he felt the chilling influence of its death-cold eyes; and marked the very texture of the folded kerchief bound about its head and chin, which wrapper he had not observed before; he was still incredulous, and fought against his senses.

"How now." said Scrooge, caustic and cold as ever. "What do you want with me?"

"Much." It was Marley's voice, no doubt about it.

"Who are you?"

"Ask me who I was."

"Who were you then?" said Scrooge, raising his voice. "You're particular – for a shade." He was going to say 'to a shade,' but substituted this, as more appropriate.

"In life I was your business partner, Jacob Marley."

"Can you – can you sit down?" asked Scrooge, looking doubtfully at him.

"I can."

"Do it, then."

Scrooge asked the question, because he didn't know whether a ghost so transparent might find himself in a condition to take a chair; and felt that in the event of its being impossible, it might involve the necessity of an embarrassing explanation. But the ghost sat down on the opposite side of the fireplace, as if he were quite used to it.

"You don't believe in me," observed the Ghost.

"I don't," said Scrooge.

"What evidence would you have of my reality beyond that of your senses?"

"I don't know," said Scrooge.

"Why do you doubt your senses?"

"Because," said Scrooge, "a little thing affects them. A slight disorder of the stomach makes them cheats. You may be an undigested bit of beef, a blot of mustard, a crumb of cheese, a fragment of an underdone potato. There's more of gravy than of grave about you, whatever you are!"

Scrooge was not much in the habit of cracking jokes, nor did he feel, in his heart, by any means waggish then. The truth is, that he tried to be smart, as a means of distracting his own attention, and keeping down his terror; for the spectre's voice disturbed the very marrow in his bones.

To sit, staring at those fixed glazed eyes in silence for a moment, would play, Scrooge felt, the very deuce with him. There was something very awful, too, in the spectre's being provided with an infernal atmosphere of its own. Scrooge could not feel it himself, but this was clearly the case; for though the Ghost sat perfectly motionless, its hair, and skirts, and tassels, were still agitated as by the hot vapour from an oven.

"You see this toothpick?" said Scrooge, returning quickly to the charge, for the reason just assigned; and wishing, though it were only for a second, to divert the vision's stony gaze from himself.

"I do," replied the Ghost.

"You are not looking at it," said Scrooge.

"But I see it," said the Ghost, "notwithstanding."

"Well," returned Scrooge, "I have but to swallow this, and

be for the rest of my days persecuted by a legion of goblins, all of my own creation. Humbug, I tell you: humbug!"

At this the spirit raised a frightful cry, and shook its chain with such a dismal and appalling noise, that Scrooge held on tight to his chair, to save himself from falling in a swoon. But how much greater was his horror, when the phantom taking off the bandage round its head, as if it were too warm to wear indoors, its lower jaw dropped down upon its breast!

Scrooge fell upon his knees, and clasped his hands before his face.

"Mercy!" he said. "Dreadful apparition, why do you trouble me?"

"Man of the worldly mind!" replied the Ghost. "Do you believe in me or not?"

"I do," said Scrooge. "I must. But why do spirits walk the earth, and why do they come to me?"

"It is required of every man," the Ghost returned, "that the spirit within him should walk abroad among his fellow-men, and travel far and wide; and if that spirit goes not forth in life, it is condemned to do so after death. It is doomed to wander through the world – oh, woe is me! – and witness what it cannot share, but might have shared on earth, and turned to happiness."

Again the spectre raised a cry, and shook its chain and wrung its shadowy hands.

"You are fettered," said Scrooge, trembling. "Tell me why?"

"I wear the chain I forged in life," replied the Ghost.

"I made it link by link, and yard by yard; I girded it on of my own free will, and of my own free will I wore it. Is its pattern strange to you?"

Scrooge trembled more and more.

"Or would you know," pursued the Ghost, "the weight and length of the strong coil you bear yourself? It was full as heavy and as long as this, seven Christmas Eves ago. You have laboured on it, since. It is a ponderous chain!"

Scrooge glanced about him on the floor, in the expectation of finding himself surrounded by some fifty or sixty fathoms of iron cable: but he could see nothing.

"Jacob," he said, imploringly. "Old Jacob Marley, tell me more. Speak comfort to me, Jacob."

"I have none to give," the Ghost replied. "It comes from other regions, Ebenezer Scrooge, and is conveyed by other ministers, to other kinds of men. Nor can I tell you what I would. A very little more is all permitted to me. I cannot rest, I cannot stay, I cannot linger anywhere. My spirit never walked beyond our counting-house – mark me! – in life my spirit never roved beyond the narrow limits of our money-changing hole; and weary journeys lie before me!"

It was a habit with Scrooge, whenever he became thoughtful, to put his hands in his breeches pockets. Pondering on what the Ghost had said, he did so now, but without lifting up his eyes, or getting off his knees.

"You must have been very slow about it, Jacob," Scrooge observed, in a businesslike manner, though with humility and deference.

"Slow!" the Ghost repeated.

"Seven years dead," mused Scrooge. "And travelling all the time?"

"The whole time," said the Ghost. "No rest, no peace. Incessant torture of remorse."

"You travel fast?" said Scrooge.

"On the wings of the wind," replied the Ghost.

"You might have got over a great quantity of ground in seven years," said Scrooge.

The Ghost, on hearing this, set up another cry, and clanked its chain so hideously in the dead silence of the night, that the Ward would have been justified in indicting it for a nuisance.

"Oh! Captive, bound, and double-ironed," cried the phantom, "not to know, that ages of incessant labour by immortal creatures, for this earth must pass into eternity before the good of which it is susceptible is all developed! Not to know that any Christian spirit working kindly in its little sphere, whatever it may be, will find its mortal life too short for its vast means of usefulness! Not to know that no space of regret can make amends for one life's opportunity misused!

Yet such was I! Oh! such was I!"

"But you were always a good man of business, Jacob," faltered Scrooge, who now began to apply this to himself.

"Business!" cried the Ghost, wringing its hands again. "Mankind was my business. The common welfare was my business; charity, mercy, forbearance, and benevolence were all my business. The dealings of my trade were but a drop of water in the comprehensive ocean of my business!"

It held up its chain at arm's length, as if that were the cause of all its unavailing grief, and flung it heavily upon the ground again.

"At this time of the rolling year," the spectre said, "I suffer most. Why did I walk through crowds of fellow-beings with my eyes turned down, and never raise them to that blessed Star which led the Wise Men to a poor abode? Were there no poor homes to which its light would have conducted me?"

Scrooge was very much dismayed to hear the spectre going on at this rate, and began to quake exceedingly.

"Hear me!" cried the Ghost. "My time is nearly gone."

"I will," said Scrooge. "But don't be hard upon me. Don't be flowery, Jacob! Pray!"

"How it is that I appear before you in a shape that you can see, I may not tell. I have sat invisible beside you many and many a day."

It was not an agreeable idea. Scrooge shivered, and wiped the perspiration from his brow.

"That is no light part of my penance," pursued the Ghost.

"I am here tonight to warn you, that you have yet a chance and hope of escaping my fate. A chance and hope of my procuring, Ebenezer."

"You were always a good friend to me," said Scrooge. "Thank'ee."

"You will be haunted," resumed the Ghost, "by Three Spirits."

Scrooge's countenance fell almost as low as the Ghost's had done.

"Is that the chance and hope you mentioned, Jacob?" he demanded, in a faltering voice.

"It is."

"I-I think I'd rather not," said Scrooge.

"Without their visits," said the Ghost, "you cannot hope to shun the path I tread. Expect the first tomorrow, when the bell tolls one."

"Couldn't I take them all at once, and have it over, Jacob?" hinted Scrooge.

"Expect the second on the next night at the same hour. The third upon the next night when the last stroke of twelve has ceased to vibrate. Look to see me no more; and look that, for your own sake, you remember what has passed between us!"

When it had said these words, the spectre took its wrapper from the table, and bound it round its head, as before. Scrooge knew this, by the smart sound its teeth made, when the jaws were brought together by the bandage. He ventured to raise his eyes again, and found his supernatural visitor confronting him in an erect attitude, with its chain wound over and about its arm.

The apparition walked backward from him; and at every step it took, the window raised itself a little, so that when the spectre reached it, it was wide open.

It beckoned Scrooge to approach, which he did. When they were within two paces of each other, Marley's Ghost held up its hand, warning him to come no nearer. Scrooge stopped.

Not so much in obedience, as in surprise and fear: for on the raising of the hand, he became sensible of confused noises in the air; incoherent sounds of lamentation and regret; wailings inexpressibly sorrowful and self-accusatory. The spectre, after listening for a moment, joined in the mournful dirge; and floated out upon the bleak, dark night.

Scrooge followed to the window: desperate in his curiosity. He looked out.

The air was filled with phantoms, wandering hither and thither in restless haste, and moaning as they went. Everyone of them wore chains like Marley's Ghost; some few (they might be guilty governments) were linked together; none were free.

Many had been personally known to Scrooge in their lives. He had been quite familiar with one old ghost, in a white waistcoat, with a monstrous iron safe attached to its ankle, who cried piteously at being unable to assist a wretched woman with an infant, whom it saw below, upon a doorstep. The misery with them all was, clearly, that they sought to interfere, for good, in human matters, and had lost the power forever.

Whether these creatures faded into mist, or mist enshrouded them, he could not tell. But they and their spirit voices faded together; and the night became as it had been when he walked home.

Scrooge closed the window, and examined the door by which the Ghost had entered. It was double locked, as he had locked it with his own hands, and the bolts were undisturbed. He tried to say "Humbug!" but stopped at the first syllable. And being, from the emotion he had undergone, or the fatigues of the day, or his glimpse of the 'invisible world', or the dull conversation of the Ghost, or the lateness of the hour, much in need of repose; went straight to bed, without undressing, and fell asleep upon the instant.

The Ship that saw a Ghost

Frank Norris

Extract

So the *Glarus* plodded and churned her way onwards.
Every day and all day the same pale blue sky and
unwinking sun bent over that moving speck. Every day
and all day the same black-blue water-world, untouched by any
known wind, smooth as a slab of syenite, colourful as an opal,
stretched out and around and beyond and before and behind us,
forever, illimitable, empty. Every day, the smoke of our fires
veiled the streaked whiteness of our wake. Every day
Hardenberg (our skipper) at noon pricked a pin hole in the
chart that hung in the wheel house, and that showed we were so
much farther into the wilderness. Every day the world of men,
of civilization, of newspapers, policemen, and street railways,

116

receded, and we steamed on alone, lost and forgotten in that silent sea.

"Jolly lot o' room to turn raound in," observed Ally Bazan, the colonial, "withaout steppin' on y'r neighbour's toes."

"We're clean, clean out o' the track of navigation," Hardenberg told him. "An' a blessed good thing for us, too. Nobody ever comes down into these waters. Ye couldn't pick no course here. Everything leads to nowhere."

"Might as well be in a bally balloon," said Strokher.

I shall not tell of the nature of the venture on which the *Glarus* was bound, further than to say it was not legitimate. It had to do with an ill thing done more than two centuries ago. There was money in the venture, but it was to be gained by a violation of metes and bounds which are better left intact.

The island towards which we were heading is associated in the minds of men with a horror. A ship had called there once, two hundred years in advance of the *Glarus* – a ship not much unlike the crank high-prowed caravel of Hudson, and her company had landed, and having accomplished the evil they had set out to do, made shift to sail away. And then, just after the palms of the island had sunk from sight below the water's edge, the unspeakable had happened. The death that was not death had arisen from out the sea and stood before the ship; and over it and the blight of the thing lay along the decks like mould, and the ship sweated in the terror of that which is yet without a name. Twenty men died in the first week, all but six in the second. These six, with the shadow of insanity upon them, made out to launch a boat, returned to the island and died there, after leaving a record of what had happened.

The six left the ship exactly as she was, sails all set, lanterns all lit – left her in the shadow of the death that was not death. The wind made at the time, they said, and as they bent to their bars, she sailed after them, for all the world like a thing refusing to abandon them or be herself abandoned, till the wind died down. Then they left her behind, and she stood there, becalmed, and watched them go. She was never heard of again.

Or was she – well, that's as may be.

But the main point of the whole affair to my notion, has always been this. The ship was the last friend of those six poor wretches who made back for the island with their poor chests of plunder. She was their guardian, as it were, would have defended and befriended them to the last; and also we, the Three Black Crows and myself, had no right under heaven, nor before the law of men, to come prying and peeping into this business – into this affair of the dead and buried past. There was sacrilege in it. We were no better than body snatchers.

When I heard the others complaining of the loneliness of our surroundings, I said nothing at first. I was no sailor man and I was on board only by tolerance. But I looked again at the maddening sameness of the horizon – the same vacant, void horizon that we had seen now for sixteen days on end, and felt in my wits and in my nerves that same formless rebellion and protest such as comes when the same note is reiterated over and over again.

The Ship that Saw a Ghost

It may seem a little thing that the mere fact of meeting with no other ship should have ground down the edge of the spirit. But let the incredulous – bound upon such a hazard as ours – sail straight into nothingness for sixteen days on end, seeing nothing but the sun, hearing nothing but the thresh of his own screw, and then put the question.

And yet, of all things, we desired no company. Stealth was our one great aim. But I think there were moments – towards the last – when the Three Crows would have welcomed even a cruiser.

On the seventh day, Hardenberg and I were forward by the cat-head adjusting the grain with some half formed intent of spearing the porpoises that of late had begun to appear under our bows, and Hardenberg had been computing the number of days we were yet to run.

"We are some five hundred odd miles off that island by now," he said, "and she's doing her thirteen knots handsome. All's well so far – but do you know, I'd just as soon raise that point o' land as soon as convenient."

"How so?" said I, bending on the line. "Expect some weather?"

"Mr Dixon," said he, giving me a curious glance, "the sea is a queer proposition, put it any ways. I've been a sea-farin' man since I was as big as a minute, and I know the sea, and what's more, the Feel o' the Sea. Now, look out yonder. Nothin', hey? Nothin' but the same ol' skyline we've watched all the way out. The glass is as steady as a steeple, and this ol' hooker, I reckon, is as sound as the day she went off the ways. But just the same, if I were to home now, a-foolin' about Gloucester way in my little dough-dish – d'ye know what? I'd put into port. I sure would. Because why? Because I got the Feel o' the Sea, Mr Dixon. I got the Feel o' the Sea."

I had heard old skippers say something of this before, and I cited to Hardenberg the experience of a skipper captain I once knew who had turned turtle in a calm sea off Trincomalee. I asked what this Feel of the Sea was warning him against just now (for on the high sea any premonition is a premonition of evil, not of good). But he was not explicit.

"I don't know," he answered moodily, and as if in great perplexity, coiling the rope as he spoke. "I don't know. There's some blame thing or other close to us, I'll bet a hat. I don't know the name of it, Mr Dixon, and I don't know the game of it, but there's a big bird in the air, just out of sight someres, and," he suddenly exclaimed, smacking his knee and leaning forward, "I – don't – like – it – one – dam' – bit."

The same thing came up in our talk in the cabin that night, after the dinner was taken off, and we settled down to tobacco. Only, at this time, Hardenberg was on duty on the bridge. It was Ally Bazan who spoke instead.

"Seems to me," he hazarded, "as haow they's somethin' or other a-goin' to bump up, pretty blyme soon. I shouldn't be surprised, naow, y'know, if we piled her up on some bally uncharted reef along o' tonight and went strite daown afore we'd had a bloomin' charnce to s'y 'So long, gen'lemen all.'"

The Ship that Saw a Ghost

He laughed as he spoke, but when, just at that moment, a pan clattered in the galley, he jumped suddenly with an oath, and looked hard about the cabin.

Then Strokher confessed to a sense of distress also. He'd been having it since day before yesterday, it seemed.

"And I put it to you the glass is lovely," he said, "so it's no blow. I guess," he continued, "we're all a bit seedy and ship sore."

And whether or not this talk worked upon my own nerves, or whether in very truth the feel of the sea had found me also, I do not know; but I do know that after dinner that night, just before going to bed, a queer sense of apprehension came upon me, and that when I had come to my stateroom, I became furiously angry with nobody in particular, because I could not at once find the matches. But here was a difference. The other men had been merely vaguely uncomfortable.

I could put a name to my uneasiness. I felt that we were being watched.

It was a strange ship's company we made after that. I speak only of the crows and myself. We carried a scant crew of stokers, and there was also a chief engineer. But we saw so little of him that he did not count. The crows and I gloomed on the quarter deck from dawn to dark: silent, irritable, working upon each other's nerves till the creak of a block would make a man jump like cold steel laid to his flesh. We quarrelled over nothing, glowered at each other for half a word, and each one of us, at different times, was at some pains to declare that never in the course of his career had he been associated with such a disagreeable trio of brutes. Yet we were always together and sought each other's company.

Only once were we all agreed, and that was when the cook, a Chinaman, spoiled a certain batch of biscuits. Unanimously we fell foul of the creature with so much vociferation as fishwives till he fled the cabin in actual fear of mishandling, leaving us suddenly seized with noisy hilarity – for the first time in a week. Hardenberg proposed a round of drinks from our single remaining case of beer. We stood up and formed an Elk's chain and then drained our glasses to each other's health.

That same evening, I remember, we all sat on the quarterdeck till late and – oddly enough – related each one his life's history up to date; and then went down to the cabin for a game of euchre before turning in.

We had left Strokher on the bridge – it was his watch – and had forgotten all about him in the interest of the game, when – I suppose it was about one in the morning – I heard him whistle long and shrill. I laid down my cards and said: "Hark!"

In the silence that followed we heard at first only the muffled lope of our engines, the cadenced snorting of the exhaust, and the ticking of Hardenberg's big watch in his waistcoat. Then from the bridge, above our deck, prolonged, intoned – a wailing cry in the night – came Strokher's voice: "Sail oh-h-h."

And the cards fell from our hands, and, like men turned to

stone, we sat looking at each other across the soiled red cloth for what seemed an immeasurably long minute. Then stumbling and swearing, in a hysteria of hurry, we gained the deck.

There was a moon, very low and reddish, but no wind. The sea beyond the taffrail was as smooth as lava, and so still that the swells from the cutwater of the *Glarus* did not break as they rolled away from the bows.

I remember that I stood staring and blinking at the empty ocean – where the moonlight lay like a painted stripe reaching to the horizon – stupid and frowning, till Hardenberg, who had gone on ahead, cried: "Not here – on the bridge!"

We joined Strokher, and as I came up the others were asking: "Where? Where?"

And there, before he had pointed, I saw – we all of us saw. And I heard Hardenberg's teeth come together like a spring trap, while Ally Bazan ducked as though to a blow, muttering: "Gord'a mercy, what nyme do ye put to a ship like that?"

And after that no one spoke for a long minute, and we stood there, moveless black shadows, huddled together for th sake of the blessed elbow touch that means so incalculably much, looking off over our port quarter.

For the ship that we saw there – oh, she was not a half-mile distant – was unlike any ship known to present day construction.

She was short, and high-pooped, and her stern, which was turned a little towards us, we could see, was set with curious windows, not unlike a house. And on either side of this stern

were two great iron cressets such as once were used to burn signal fires in. She had three masts with mighty yards swung 'thwart ship, but bare of all sails save a few rotting streamers. Here and there about her a tangled mass of rigging drooped and sagged.

And there she lay, in the red eye of the setting moon, in that solitary ocean, shadowy, antique, forlorn, a thing the most abandoned, the most sinister I ever remember to have seen.

Then Strokher began to explain volubly and with many repetitions.

"A derelict, of course. I was asleep; yes I was asleep. Gross neglect of duty. And we worked up to her. When I woke, why – you see, when I woke, there she was," he gave a weak little laugh, "and – and now, why, there she is, you see. I turned around and saw her sudden like – when I woke up, that is."

He laughed again, and as he laughed, the engines far below our feet gave a sudden hiccough. Something crashed and struck the ship's sides till we lurched as we stood. There was a shriek of steam, a shout – and then silence.

The noise of the machinery ceased; the *Glarus* slid through the still water, moving only by her own decreasing momentum.

Hardenberg sang, "Stand by!" and called down the tube to the engine room.

"What's up?"

I was standing close enough to him to hear the answer in a small faint voice:

"Shaft gone, sir."

"Broke?"

"Yes, sir."

Hardenberg faced about. "Come below. We must talk."

I do not think any of us cast a glance at the other ship again. Certainly I kept my eyes away from her. But as we started down the companionway, I laid my hand on Strokher's shoulder. I looked him straight between the eyes as I asked: "*Were* you asleep? *Is* that why you saw her so suddenly?"

It is now five years since I asked the question. I am still waiting for Strokher's answer.

Well, our shaft was broken. We went down into the engine room and saw the jagged fracture that was the symbol of our broken hopes. And in the course of the next five minutes conversation with the chief, we found that there was to be no mending of it. We said nothing about the mishap coinciding with the appearance of the ship. But I know we did not consider the break with any degree of surprise after a few moments.

We came slowly up from the engine room and sat down at the cabin table in a dispirited fashion.

"Now what?" said Hardenberg, by way of beginning.

Nobody answered at first.

It was by now three in the morning. I recall it all perfectly. The ports opposite where I sat were open and I could see. The moon was all but full set. The dawn was coming up with a copper murkiness over the edge of the world. All the stars were yet out. The sea, for all the red moon and copper dawn, was grey, and there, less than half a mile away, still lay our consort.

I could see her through the portholes with each slow careening of the *Glarus*.

"I vote for the island," cried Ally Bazan, "shaft or no shaft. We rigs a bit o' syle, y'know," – and thereat the discussion began.

For upwards of two hours it raged, with loud words and shaken forefingers, and great noisy bangings of the table, and how it would have ended I do not know, but at last – it was then maybe five in the morning – the lookout passed word down to the cabin: "Will you come on deck, gentlemen?" It was the mate who spoke, and the man was shaken – I could see that – to the very vitals of him.

We stared at one another, and I watched little Ally Bazan go slowly white to the lips. And even then no word of the Ship, except as it might be this from Hardenberg: "What is it? Good God Almighty, I'm no coward, but this thing is getting one too many for me." Then without further speech he went on deck.

The air was cool. The sun was not yet up. It was that strange, queer mid-period between dark and dawn, when the night is over and the day not yet come, just the grey that is neither light nor dark, the dim dead blink as of the refracted light from extinct worlds.

We stood at the rail. We did not speak, we stood watching. It was so still that the drip of steam from some loosened pipe far below was plainly audible, and it sounded in that lifeless, silent greyness, like – God knows what – a death tick.

"You see," said the mate, speaking just above a whisper,

"there's no mistake about it. She is moving – this way."

"Oh, a current, of course," Strokher tried to say cheerfully, "sets her towards us."

Would the morning never come?

Ally Bazan – his parents were Catholic – began to mutter to himself.

Then Hardenberg spoke aloud.

"I particularly don't want – that – out – there – to cross our bows. I don't want it to come to that. We must get some sails on her."

"And I put it to you as man to man," said Strokher, "where might be your wind?"

He was right. The *Glarus* floated in absolute calm. On all that slab of ocean nothing moved but the dead ship.

She came on slowly; her bows, the high clumsy bows pointed towards us, the water turning from her forefoot. She came on; she was near at hand. We saw her plainly – saw the rotted planks, the crumbling rigging, the rust-corroded metalwork, the broken rail, the gaping deck – and I could imagine that the clean water broke away from her sides in refluent wavelets as though in recoil from a thing unclean. She made no sound. No single thing stirred aboard the hulk of her – but she moved.

We were helpless. The *Glarus* could stir no boat in any direction; we were chained to the spot. Nobody had thought to put out our lights, and they still burned on through the dawn, strangely out of place in their red and green garishness.

The Ship that Saw a Ghost

And in the silence of that empty ocean, in that queer half-light between dawn and day, at six o'clock, silent as the settling of the dead to the bottomless bottom of the ocean, grey as fog, lonely, blind, soulless, voiceless, the dead ship crossed our bows.

I do not know how long after this the ship disappeared, or what was the time of day when we at last pulled ourselves together. But we came to some sort of decision at last. This was to go on – under sail. We were too close to the island now to turn back for – for a broken shaft.

The afternoon was spent fitting on the sails to her, and when after nightfall the wind at length came up fresh and favourable, I believe we all felt heartened and a deal more hardy – until the last canvass went aloft, and Hardenberg took the wheel.

We had drifted a good deal since the morning, and the bows of the *Glarus* were pointed homewards, but as soon as the breeze blew strong enough to get steerage way, Hardenberg put the wheel over, and headed for the island again.

We had not gone on this course half an hour – no, not twenty minutes – before the wind shifted a whole quarter of the compass and took the *Glarus* square in the teeth, so that there was nothing for it but to tack. And then the strangest thing befell.

I will make allowance for the fact that there was no centre board nor keel to speak of to the *Glarus*. I will admit that the sails upon a 900-tonne freighter are not calculated to speed her, nor steady her. I will even admit the possibility of a current that set from the island towards us. All this may be true, yet the *Glarus* should have advanced. We should have made a wake.

Instead of this our trusty old boat was – what shall I say?

I will say that no man may thoroughly understand a ship – after all. I will say that new ships are cranky and unsteady, that old and seasoned ships have their little crotchets, their little fussinesses that their skippers must learn and humour if they are to get anything out of them; that even the best ships may sulk at times, shirk their work, grow unstable, perverse, and refuse to answer helm and handling. And I will say that some ships that for years have sailed blue water as soberly and as docilely as a street-car horse has plodded the treadmill of the 'tween-tracks, have been known to balk, as stubbornly and as conclusively as any old Bay Billy that ever wore a bell. I know this has happened, because I have seen it. I saw, for instance, the *Glarus* do it.

Quite literally and truly we could do nothing with her. We will say, if you like, that that great jar and wrench when the shaft gave way shook her and crippled her. It is true, however, that whatever the cause may have been, we could not force her towards the island.

For three days and three nights we tried it. And the *Glarus* heaved and plunged and shook herself just as you have seen a horse plunge and rear when his rider tries to force him at the steam-roller.

The Ship that Saw a Ghost

I tell you I could feel the fabric of her tremble and shudder from bow to stern post, as though she were in a storm; I tell you she fell off from the wind, and broad-on drifted back from her course till the sensation of her shrinking was as plain as her own staring lights and a thing pitiful to see.

We rowelled her and we crowded sail upon her, and we coaxed and bullied and humoured her, till the Three Crows, their fortune only a plain sail two days ahead, raved and swore like insensate brutes, or shall we say like *mahouts*, trying to drive their stricken elephant upon the tiger – and all to no purpose. "Damn the damned current and the damned luck and the damned shaft and all," Hardenberg would exclaim, as from the wheel he would watch the *Glarus* falling off. "Go on, you old hooker – you tub of junk! My God, you'd think she was scared!"

Perhaps the *Glarus* was scared; that point is debatable. But it was beyond doubt or debate that Hardenberg was scared.

A ship that will not obey is only one degree less terrible than a mutinous crew. And we were in a fair way to have both. The stokers whom we had impressed into duty as A.B.'s, were of course superstitious. They had seen – what we had seen and they knew how the *Glarus* was acting and it was only a question of time before they got out of hand.

That was the end. We held a final conference in the cabin and decided that there was no help for it – we must turn back.

And back we accordingly turned, and at once the wind followed us, and the 'current' helped us, and the water churned under the forefoot of the *Glarus*, and the wake whitened under her stern, and the log-line ran out from the rail and strained back as the ship worked homewards.

We had never a mishap from the time we finally swung her about; and, considering the circumstances, the voyage back to San Francisco was propitious.

But an incident happened just after we had started back. We were perhaps some five miles on the homeward track. It was early evening and Strokher had the watch. At about seven o'clock he called me up on the bridge. "See her?" he said.

And there, far behind us, in the shadow of the twilight, loomed the other ship again, desolate, lonely beyond words. We were leaving her rapidly astern. Strokher and I stood looking at her till she dwindled to a dot. Then Strokher said: "She's on post again."

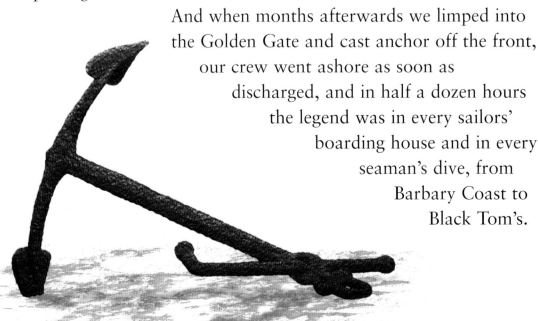

And when months afterwards we limped into the Golden Gate and cast anchor off the front, our crew went ashore as soon as discharged, and in half a dozen hours the legend was in every sailors' boarding house and in every seaman's dive, from Barbary Coast to Black Tom's.

The Ship that Saw a Ghost

It is still there, and that is why no pilot will take the *Glarus* out, no captain will navigate her, no stoker feed her fires, no sailor walk her decks. The *Glarus* is suspect. She will never smell blue water again. She has seen a ghost.

The Picture of Dorian Gray

Oscar Wilde

Extract

For some reason or other, the house was crowded that night, and the fat manager who met them at the door was beaming from ear to ear with an oily tremulous smile. He escorted them to their box with a sort of pompous humility, waving his fat jewelled hands and talking at the top of his voice. Dorian Gray loathed him more than ever. He felt as if he had come to look for Miranda and had been met by Caliban. Lord Henry, upon the other hand, rather liked him. At least he declared he did, and insisted on shaking him by the hand and assuring him that he was proud to meet a man who had discovered a real genius and gone bankrupt over a poet. Hallward amused himself with watching the faces in the pit. The heat was terribly oppressive, and the huge sunlight flamed like a monstrous dahlia with petals of yellow fire. The youths in the gallery had taken off their coats and waistcoats and hung them over the side. The sound of the popping of corks came from the bar.

"What a place to find one's divinity in!" said Lord Henry.

"Yes!" answered Dorian Gray. "It was here I found her, and she is divine beyond all living things. When she acts, you will forget everything. These common rough people, with their coarse faces and brutal gestures, become quite different when she is on the stage. They sit silently and watch her. They weep and laugh as she wills them to do. She makes them as responsive as a violin. She spiritualizes them, and one feels that they are of the same flesh and blood as one's self."

"The same flesh and blood as one's self! Oh, I hope not!" exclaimed Lord Henry, who was scanning the occupants of the gallery through his opera-glass.

"Don't pay any attention to him, Dorian," said the painter. "I understand what you mean, and I believe in this girl. Anyone you love must be marvellous. If this girl can give a soul to those who have lived without one, if she can create the sense of beauty in people whose lives have been sordid and ugly, if she can strip them of their selfishness and lend them tears for sorrows that are not their own, she is worthy of all your adoration. This marriage is quite right. I did not think so at first, but I admit it now. The gods made Sibyl Vane for you. Without her you would have been incomplete."

"Thanks, Basil," answered Dorian Gray, pressing his hand.

"I knew that you would understand me. Harry is so cynical, he terrifies me. But here is the orchestra. It is quite dreadful, but it only lasts for about five minutes. Then the curtain rises, and you will see the girl to whom I am going to give all my life, to whom I have given everything that is good in me."

A quarter of an hour afterwards, amidst an extraordinary turmoil of applause, Sibyl Vane stepped onto the stage. Yes, she was certainly lovely to look at – one of the loveliest creatures, Lord Henry thought, that he had ever seen. There was something of the fawn in her shy grace and startled eyes. A faint blush, like the shadow of a rose in a mirror of silver, came to her cheeks as she glanced at the crowded, enthusiastic house. She stepped back a few paces and her lips seemed to tremble. Basil Hallward leapt to his feet and began to applaud. Lord Henry peered through his glasses, murmuring, "Charming! charming!"

The scene was the hall of Capulet's house, and Romeo in his pilgrim's dress had entered with Mercutio and his other friends. The band, such as it was, struck up a few bars of music, and the dance began. Through the crowd of ungainly, shabbily dressed actors, Sibyl Vane moved like a creature from a finer world. The curves of her throat were the curves of a white lily. Her hands seemed to be made of cool ivory.

Yet she was curiously listless. She showed no sign of joy when her eyes rested on Romeo. The few words she had to speak were spoken in a thoroughly artificial manner. The voice was exquisite, but from the point of view of tone it was absolutely false. It was wrong in colour. It took away all the life from the verse. It made the passion unreal.

Dorian Gray grew pale as he watched her. He was puzzled and anxious. Neither of his friends dared to say anything to him. She seemed to them to be absolutely incompetent. They were horribly disappointed.

Yet they felt that the true test of any Juliet is the balcony scene of the second act. If she failed there, there was nothing in her.

She looked charming as she came out in the moonlight. That could not be denied. But the staginess of her acting was unbearable, and grew worse as she went on. Her gestures became absurdly artificial. She overemphasized everything that she had to say. The beautiful passage:

Thou knowest the mask of night is on my face,
Else would a maiden blush bepaint my cheek
For that which thou hast heard me speak tonight

was declaimed with the painful precision of a schoolgirl who has been taught to recite by some second-rate professor of elocution. When she leaned over the balcony and came to those wonderful lines:

Although I joy in thee,
I have no joy of this contract to-night:
It is too rash, too unadvised, too sudden;
Too like the lightning, which doth cease to be
Ere one can say, "It lightens." Sweet, goodnight!
This bud of love by summer's ripening breath
May prove a beauteous flower when next we meet

she spoke the words as though they conveyed no meaning to her. It was not nervousness. Indeed, so far from being nervous, she was absolutely self-contained. It was simply bad art. She was a complete failure.

Even the common uneducated audience of the pit and gallery lost their interest in the play. They got restless, and began to talk loudly and to whistle. The manager, who was standing at the back of the dress circle, stamped and swore with rage. The only person unmoved was the girl herself.

When the second act was over, there came a storm of hisses, and Lord Henry got up from his chair and put on his coat. "She is quite beautiful, Dorian," he said, "but she can't act. Let us go."

"I am going to see the play through," answered the lad, in a hard bitter voice. "I am awfully sorry that I have made you waste an evening, Harry. I apologize to you both."

"My dear Dorian, I should think Miss Vane was ill," interrupted Hallward. "We will come some other night."

"I wish she were ill," he rejoined. "But she seems to me to be simply callous and cold. She has entirely altered. Last night she was a great artist. This evening she is merely a commonplace mediocre actress."

"Don't talk like that about anyone you love, Dorian. Love is a more wonderful thing than art."

"They are both simply forms of imitation," remarked Lord Henry. "But do let us go. Dorian, you must not stay here any longer. It is not good for one's morals to see bad acting. Besides, I don't suppose you will want your wife to act, so what does it matter if she plays Juliet like a wooden doll? She is very lovely, and if she knows as little about life as she does about acting, she will be a delightful experience. Good heavens, my dear boy, don't look so tragic! The secret of remaining young is never to have an emotion that is unbecoming. Come to the club with

Basil and myself. We will smoke cigarettes and drink to the beauty of Sibyl Vane"

"Go away, Harry," cried the lad. "I want to be alone. Basil, you must go. Ah! Can't you see that my heart is breaking?" The hot tears came to his eyes. His lips trembled, and rushing to the back of the box, he leant up against the wall, hiding his face in his hands.

"Let us go, Basil," said Lord Henry with a strange tenderness in his voice, and the two men passed out together.

A few moments afterwards the footlights flared up and the curtain rose on the third act. Dorian Gray went back to his seat. He looked pale, and proud, and indifferent. The play dragged on. Half of the audience went out, tramping in heavy boots and laughing. The whole thing was a fiasco. The last act was played to almost empty benches. The curtain went down groans.

As soon as it was over, Dorian Gray rushed behind the scenes into the greenroom. The girl was standing there alone, with a look of triumph on her face. There was a radiance about her. Her parted lips were smiling over some secret of their own.

When he entered, she looked at him, and an expression of joy came over her. "How badly I acted tonight," she cried.

"Horribly!" he answered, gazing at her in amazement. "Horribly! It was dreadful. Are you ill? You have no idea what it was. You have no idea what I suffered."

The girl smiled. "Dorian," she answered, lingering over his name with long-drawn music in her voice, as though it were sweeter than honey to the red petals of her mouth. "Dorian, you should have understood. You understand now, don't you?"

"Understand what?" he asked, angrily.

"Why I was so bad tonight. Why I shall always be bad. Why I shall never act well again."

He shrugged his shoulders. "You are ill, I suppose. When you are ill you shouldn't act. You make yourself ridiculous. My friends were bored. I was bored."

She seemed not to listen to him. She was transfigured with joy. An ecstasy of happiness dominated her.

"Dorian, Dorian," she cried, "before I knew you, acting was the one reality of my life. It was only in the theatre that I lived. I thought that it was all true. I was Rosalind one night and Portia the other. The joy of Beatrice was my joy, and the sorrows of Cordelia were mine also. I believed in everything. The common people who acted with me seemed to me to be godlike. The painted scenes were my world. I knew nothing but shadows, and I thought them real. You came – oh, my beautiful love! – and you freed my soul from prison. You taught me what reality really is. Tonight, for the first time in my life, I saw through the hollowness, the sham, the silliness of the empty pageant in which I had always played. Tonight, for the first time, I became conscious that the Romeo was hideous and old and painted, that the moonlight in the orchard was false, that the scenery was vulgar, and that the words I had to speak were unreal, were not my words, were not what I wanted to say. You had brought me something higher, something of which all art is but a reflection. You had made me understand what love really is. My love! My love! Prince Charming! Prince of life! I have grown sick of shadows. You are more to me than all art can ever be. What have I to do with the puppets of a play? When I came on to-night, I could not understand how it was that everything had gone from me. I thought that I was going to be wonderful. I found that I could do nothing. Suddenly it dawned on my soul what it all meant. The knowledge was exquisite to me. I heard them hissing, and I smiled. What could they know of love such as ours? Take me away, Dorian – take me away with you, where we can be quite alone. I hate the stage. I might mimic a passion that I do not feel, but I cannot mimic one that burns me like fire. Oh, Dorian, Dorian, you understand now what it signifies? Even if I could do it, it would be profanation for me to play at being in love. You have made me see that."

He flung himself down on the sofa and turned away his face. "You have killed my love," he muttered.

She looked at him in wonder and laughed. He made no answer. She came across to him, and with her little fingers stroked his hair. She knelt down and pressed his hands to her lips. He drew them away, and a shudder ran through him.

Then he leapt up and went to the door. "Yes," he cried, "you have killed my love. You used to stir my imagination. Now you don't even stir my curiosity. You simply produce no effect. I loved you because you were marvellous, because you had genius and intellect, because you realized the dreams of great poets and gave shape and substance to the shadows of art. You have thrown it all away. You are shallow and stupid. My

God! How mad I was to love you! What a fool I have been! You are nothing to me now. I will never see you again. I will never think of you. I will never mention your name. You don't know what you were to me, once. Why, once . . . Oh, I can't bear to think of it! I wish I had never laid eyes upon you! You have spoiled the romance of my life. How little you can know of love, if

you say it mars your art! Without your art, you are nothing. I would have made you famous, splendid, magnificent. The world would have worshipped you, and you would have borne my name. What are you now? A third-rate actress with a pretty face."

The girl grew white, and trembled. She clenched her hands together, and her voice seemed to catch in her throat. "You are not serious, Dorian?" she murmured. "You are acting."

"Acting! I leave that to you. You do it so well," he

answered, and there was a heavy and now unmistakable bitterness in his voice.

She rose from her knees and, with a piteous expression of pain in her face, came across the room to him. She put her hand upon his arm and looked into his eyes. He thrust her back. "Don't touch me!" he cried.

A low moan broke from her, and she flung herself at his feet and lay there like a trampled flower. "Dorian, Dorian, don't leave me!" she whispered. "I am so sorry I didn't act well. I was thinking of you all the time. But I will try – indeed, I will try. It came so suddenly across me, my love for you. I think I should never have known it if you had not kissed me – if we had not kissed each other. Kiss me again, my love. Don't go away from me. I couldn't bear it. Oh! don't go away from me. My brother . . . No; never mind. He didn't mean it. He was in jest. . . . But you, oh! Can't you forgive me for tonight? I will work so hard and try to improve. Don't be cruel to me, because I love you better than anything in the world. After all, it is only once that I have not pleased you. But you are quite right, Dorian. I should have shown myself more of an artist. It was foolish of me, and yet I couldn't help it. Oh, don't leave me, don't leave me." A fit of passionate sobbing choked her. She crouched on the floor like a wounded thing, and Dorian Gray, with his beautiful eyes, looked down at her, and his chiselled lips curled in exquisite disdain. There is always something ridiculous about the emotions of people whom one has ceased to love. Sibyl Vane seemed to him to be absurdly melodramatic. Her tears and sobs annoyed him.

"I am going," he said at last, in his calm clear voice. "I don't wish to be unkind, but I can't see you again. You have disappointed me."

She wept silently, and made no answer, but crept nearer. Her little hands stretched blindly out, and appeared to be seeking for him. He turned on his heel and left the room. In a few moments he was out of the theatre.

Where he went to he hardly knew. He remembered wandering through dimly lit streets, past gaunt, black-shadowed archways and evil-looking houses. Women with hoarse voices and harsh

laughter had called after him. Drunkards had reeled by, cursing and chattering to themselves like monstrous apes. He had seen grotesque children huddled upon door steps, and heard shrieks and oaths from gloomy courts.

As the dawn was just breaking, he found himself close to Covent Garden. The darkness lifted, and, flushed with faint fires, the sky hollowed itself into a perfect pearl. Huge carts filled with nodding lilies rumbled slowly down the polished empty street. The air was heavy with the perfume of the flowers, and their beauty seemed to soothe his pain. He followed into the market and watched the men unloading their waggons. A white-smocked carter offered him some cherries. He thanked him, wondered why he refused to accept any money for them, and began to eat them listlessly. They had been plucked at midnight, and the coldness of the moon had entered into them. A long line of boys carrying crates of striped tulips, and of yellow and red roses, filed in front of him, threading their way through the huge, jade-green piles of vegetables. Under the portico, with its grey, sun-bleached pillars, loitered a troop of draggled bare-headed girls, waiting for the auction to be over. Others crowded round the swinging doors of the coffee house in the piazza. The heavy cart-horses slipped and stamped upon the rough stones, shaking their bells and trappings. Some of the drivers were lying asleep on a pile of sacks. Iris-necked and pink-footed, the pigeons ran about picking up seeds.

After a little while, he hailed a hansom and drove home. For a few moments he loitered upon the doorstep, looking round at the silent square, with its blank, close-shuttered windows and its staring blinds. The sky was pure opal now, and the roofs of the houses glistened like silver against it. From some chimney opposite a thin wreath of smoke was rising. It curled, a violet riband, through the nacre-coloured air.

In the huge gilt Venetian lantern, spoil of some Doge's barge, that hung from the ceiling of the great, oak-panelled hall of entrance, lights were still burning from three flickering jets: thin blue petals of flame they seemed, rimmed with white fire. He turned them out and, having thrown his hat and cape on the table, passed through the library towards the door of his bedroom, a large octagonal chamber on the ground floor that, in his new-born feeling for luxury, he had just had decorated for himself and hung with some curious Renaissance tapestries that had been discovered stored in a disused attic at Selby Royal. As he was turning the handle of the door, his eye fell upon the portrait Basil Hallward had painted of him. He started back as if in surprise. Then he went on into his own room, looking somewhat puzzled. After he had taken the button hole out of his coat, he seemed to hesitate. Finally, he came back, went over to the picture, and examined it. In the dim arrested light that struggled through the cream-coloured silk blinds, the face appeared to him to be a little changed. The expression looked different. One would have said that there was a touch of cruelty in the mouth. It was certainly strange.

He turned round and, walking to the window, drew up the blind. The bright dawn flooded the room and swept the fantastic shadows into dusky corners, where they lay shuddering. But the strange expression that he had noticed in the face of the portrait seemed to linger there, to be more intensified even. The quivering ardent sunlight showed him the lines of cruelty round the mouth as clearly as if he had been looking into a mirror after he had done some dreadful thing.

He winced and, taking up from the table an oval glass framed in ivory Cupids – one of Lord Henry's many presents to him – glanced hurriedly into its polished depths. No line like that warped his red lips. What did it mean?

He rubbed his eyes, and came close to the picture, and examined it again. There were no signs of any change when he looked into the actual painting, and yet there was no doubt that the whole expression had altered. It was not a mere fancy of his own. The thing was horribly apparent.

He threw himself into a chair and began to think. Suddenly there flashed across his mind what he had said in Basil Hallward's studio the day the picture had been finished. Yes, he remembered it perfectly. He had uttered a mad wish that he himself might remain young, and the portrait grow old; that his own beauty might be untarnished, and the face on the canvas bear the burden of his passions and his sins; that the painted image might be seared with the lines of suffering and thought, and that he might keep all the delicate bloom and loveliness of his then just conscious boyhood. Surely his wish had not been fulfilled? Such things were impossible. It seemed monstrous even to think of them. And, yet, there was the picture before him, with the touch of cruelty in the mouth that had not been there before.

Cruelty! Had he been cruel? It was the girl's fault, not his. He had dreamed of her as a great artist, had given his love to her because he had thought her great. Then she had disappointed him. She had been shallow and unworthy. And, yet, a feeling of infinite regret came over him, as he thought of her lying at his feet sobbing like a little child. He remembered with what callousness he had watched her. Why had he been made like that? Why had such a soul been given to him? But he had suffered also. During the three terrible hours that the play had lasted, he had lived centuries of pain, aeon upon aeon of torture. His life was well worth hers. She had marred him for a moment, if he had wounded her for an age. Besides, women were better suited to bear sorrow than men. They lived on their emotions. They only thought of their emotions. When they took lovers, it was merely to have someone with whom they could have scenes. Lord Henry had told him that, and Lord Henry knew what women were. Why should he trouble about Sibyl Vane? She was nothing to him now.

But the picture? What was he to say of that? It held the secret of his life, and told his story. It had taught him to love his own beauty. Would it teach him to loathe his own soul? Would he ever look at it again?

No; it was merely an illusion wrought on the troubled senses. The horrible night that he had passed had left phantoms behind it. Yet it was watching him, with its beautiful marred face and its cruel smile. Its bright hair gleamed in the early sunlight. Its blue eyes met his own. A sense of infinite pity, not for himself, but for the painted image of himself, came over him. It had altered already, and would alter more. Its gold would wither into grey. Its red and white roses would die. For every sin that he committed, a stain would fleck and wreck its fairness. But he would not sin again. The picture, changed or unchanged, would be to him the visible emblem of conscience, and would enable him to would resist temptation. He would not see Lord Henry any more – would not, at any rate, listen to those subtle poisonous theories that in Basil Hallward's garden had first stirred within him the passion for impossible things. He would go back to Sibyl Vane, try to make her amends, marry her if she would have him, and try to love her again. Yes, it was his duty to do so. She must have suffered far more than he had. The poor child! He had been selfish and cruel to her. The fascination that she had once exercised over him would return.

He got up from his chair and drew a large screen right in front of the portrait, shuddering as he glanced at it. "How horrible!" he murmured to himself, and he walked across to the window and opened it.

When he stepped out onto the grass, he drew a long, deep breath. He could think only of Sibyl. A faint echo of his love had begun to come back to him. He repeated her name over and over again. The birds that were singing in the dew-drenched garden seemed to be telling the flowers about her.

It was long past noon when he awoke. His valet had crept several times on tiptoe into the room to see if he was stirring, and had wondered what made his young master sleep so late. Finally his bell sounded, and Victor came in softly with a cup of tea, and a pile of letters, on a small tray, and drew back the olive-satin curtains, with their shimmering blue lining, that hung in front of the three tall windows.

"*Monsieur* has slept well this morning," he said, smiling.

"What o'clock is it, Victor?" asked Dorian Gray drowsily.

"One hour and a quarter, *monsieur*."

How late it was! He sat up, and having sipped some tea, turned over his letters. One of them was from Lord Henry, and had been brought by hand that morning. He hesitated for a moment, and then put it aside. The others he opened listlessly. They contained the usual collection of cards, invitations to dinner, tickets for private views, programmes of charity concerts, and the like that are showered on fashionable young men every morning during the season.

After about ten minutes he got up, and throwing on an elaborate dressing-gown of silk-embroidered cashmere wool, passed into the onyx-paved bathroom. The cool water refreshed him after his long sleep. He seemed to have forgotten all that he had gone through. A dim sense of having taken part in some strange tragedy came to him once or twice, but there was the unreality of a dream about it.

As soon as he was dressed, he went into the library and sat down to a light French breakfast that had been laid out for him on a small round table close to the open window. It was an exquisite day. The warm air seemed laden with spices. A bee flew in and buzzed round the blue-dragon bowl that, filled with roses, stood before him.

Suddenly his eye fell on the screen that he had placed in front of the portrait, and he started.

"Too cold for *monsieur*?" asked his valet, putting an omelette on the table. "I shut the window?"

Dorian shook his head. "I am not cold," he murmured.

Was it all true? Had the portrait really changed? Or had it been simply his own imagination that had made him see a look of evil where there had been a look of joy? The thing was absurd. It would serve as a tale to tell Basil some day. It would make him smile.

And, yet, how vivid was his recollection of the whole thing! First in the dim twilight, and then in the bright dawn, he had seen the touch of cruelty round the warped lips. He almost dreaded his valet leaving the room. He knew that when he was alone he would have to examine the portrait. He was afraid of certainty. As the door was closing behind him, he called him back. The man stood waiting for his orders. Dorian looked at him for a moment. "I am not at home to anyone, Victor," he said with a sigh. The man bowed and retired.

Then he rose from the table, lit a cigarette, and flung himself down on a luxuriously cushioned couch that stood facing the screen. The screen was an old one, of gilt Spanish leather, stamped and wrought with a rather florid Louis-Quatorze pattern. He scanned it curiously, wondering if ever before it had concealed the secret of a man's life.

Should he move it aside, after all? Why not let it stay there? What was the use of knowing? If the thing was true, it was terrible. If it was not true, why trouble about it? But what if, by some fate or deadlier chance, eyes other than his spied behind and saw the horrible change? What should he do if Basil Hallward came and asked to look at his own picture? Basil would be sure to do that. No; the thing had to be examined. Anything would be better than this dreadful state of doubt.

He got up and locked both doors. At least he would be alone when he looked upon the mask of his shame. Then he drew the screen aside and saw himself face to face. It was perfectly true, no one could deny the fact that the potrait had altered.

As he often remembered afterwards, and always with no small wonder, he found himself at first gazing at the portrait with a feeling of almost scientific interest. That such a change should have taken place was incredible to him. And yet it was a fact. Was there some subtle affinity between the chemical atoms that shaped themselves into form and colour on the canvas and the soul that was within him? Could it be that what that soul thought, they realized? That what it dreamed, they made true? Or was there some other, more terrible reason? He shuddered, and felt afraid, and, going back to the couch, lay there, gazing at the picture in sickened horror.

One thing, however, he felt that it had done for him. It had made him conscious how unjust, how cruel, he had been to Sibyl Vane. It was not too late to make reparation for that. She could still be his wife. His unreal and selfish love would yield to some higher influence, would be transformed into some nobler passion, and the portrait that Basil Hallward had painted of him would be a guide to him through life, would be to him what holiness is to some, and conscience to others. There were opiates for remorse, drugs that could lull the moral sense to sleep. But here was a visible symbol of the degradation of sin.

Three o'clock struck, and four, and the half-hour rang its double chime, but still Dorian Gray did not stir. He did not know what to do, or what to think. Finally, he went over to the table and wrote a passionate letter to the girl he had loved, imploring her forgiveness and accusing himself of madness. He covered page after page with wild words of sorrow and wilder words of pain. There is a luxury in self-reproach. When we blame ourselves, we feel that no one else has a right to blame us. It is the confession, not the priest, that gives us absolution. When Dorian had finished the letter, he felt comforted and that he had been forgiven.

Suddenly there came a knock to the door, and he heard Lord Henry's voice outside. "My dear boy, I must see you."

He made no answer at first. The knocking still continued. Yes, it was better to let Lord Henry in, and to explain to him the new life he was going to lead. He would be firm and not listen to his friend's talk, he would explain his new plan to him and make him understand. Dorian jumped up, drew the screen across the picture, and unlocked the door.

"I am so sorry for it all, Dorian," said Lord Henry as he entered. "But you must not think too much about it."

"Do you mean about Sibyl Vane?" asked the lad.

"Yes, of course," answered Lord Henry, sinking into a chair, "It is dreadful, from one point of view, but it was not your fault. Did you go behind and see her, after the play was over?"

"Yes."

"I felt sure you had. Did you make a scene with her?"

"I was brutal. But it is all right now. I am not sorry for anything that has happened. It has taught me to know better."

"Ah, Dorian, I am so glad you take it in that way!"

"I am perfectly happy now." Said Dorian, "I know what conscience is, to begin with. It is not what you told me it was. It is the divinest thing in us. Don't sneer Harry, I want to be good. I can't bear the idea of my soul being hideous."

"A very charming artistic basis for ethics, Dorian! I congratulate you on it. But how are you going to begin?"

"By marrying Sibyl Vane."

"Marrying Sibyl Vane!" cried Lord Henry, standing up and looking at him in perplexed amazement. "But, my dear Dorian—"

"Yes, Henry, I know what you are going to say. Something dreadful about marriage. I am not going to break my word. She is to be my wife."

"Your wife! Dorian! Didn't you get my letter?"

"Your letter? Oh, yes, I have not read it yet, Henry. I was

afraid there might be something in it that I wouldn't like. It is over there if you wish to read it to me now."

"You know nothing then?"

"What do you mean?"

Lord Henry walked across the room, and sitting down by Dorian Gray, took both his hands in his own and held them tightly. "Dorian," he said, "my letter – don't be frightened – was to tell you that Sibyl Vane is dead."

Ghosts that have Haunted Me

J K Bangs
Extract

It happened last Christmas, in my own home. I had provided as a little surprise for my wife a complete new solid silver service marked with her initials. The tree had been prepared for the children, and all had retired save myself. I had lingered later than the others to put the silver service under the tree, where its happy recipient would find it when she went to the tree with the little ones the next morning. It made a magnificent display: the two dozen of each kind of spoon, the forks, the knives, the coffee pot, water urn, and all; the salvers, the vegetable dishes, olive forks, cheese scoops, and other dazzling attributes of a complete service, not to go into details, presented a fairly scintillating picture which would have made me gasp if I had not, at the moment when my own breath began to catch, heard another gasp in the corner immediately behind me. Turning about quickly to see whence it came, I observed a dark figure in the pale light of the moon which streamed in through the window.

"Who are you?" I cried, starting back, the physical symptoms of a ghostly presence manifesting themselves as usual.

"I am the ghost of one long gone before," was the reply, in sepulchral tones.

I breathed a sigh of relief, for I had for a moment feared it was a burglar.

"Oh!" I said. "You gave me a start at first. I was afraid you were a material thing come to rob me." Then turning towards the tree, I observed, with a wave of the hand, "Fine layout, eh?"

"Beautiful," he said, hollowly. "Yet not so beautiful as things I've seen in realms beyond your ken."

And then he set about telling me of the beautiful gold and silverware they used in the Elysian Fields, and I must confess Monte Cristo would have had a hard time, with Sinbad the Sailor to help, to surpass the picture of royal magnificence the spectre drew. I stood enthralled until, even as he was talking, the clock struck three, when he rose up, and moving slowly across the floor, barely visible, murmured regretfully that he must be off, with which he faded away down the back stairs. I pulled my nerves, which were getting rather strained, together again, and went to bed.

Next morning, every bit of that silverware was gone; and, what is more, three weeks later I found the ghost's picture in the Rogue's Gallery in New York as that of the cleverest sneak-thief in the country.

All of which, let me say to you, dear reader, in conclusion, proves that when you are dealing with ghosts you mustn't give up all your physical resources until you have definitely ascertained that the thing by which you are confronted, horrid or otherwise, is a ghost, and not an all too material rogue with a light step, and a commodious jute bag for plunder concealed beneath his coat.

"How to tell a ghost?" you ask.

Well, as an eminent master of fiction frequently observes in his writings" that is another story, which I shall hope some day to tell for your instruction and my own aggrandisement.

The Strange Case of Dr Jekyll and Mr Hyde

Robert Louis Stevenson
Extract

Twelve o'clock had scarce rung out over London, ere the knocker sounded very gently on the door. I went myself at the summons, and found a small man crouching against the pillars of the portico.

"Are you come from Dr Jekyll?" I asked.

He told me 'yes' by a constrained gesture, and when I had

bidden him enter, he did not obey me without a searching backward glance into the darkness of the square. There was a policeman not far off, advancing with his bull's eye open; and at the sight, I thought my visitor started and made greater haste.

These particulars struck me, I confess, disagreeably; and as I followed him into the bright light of the consulting room, I kept my hand ready on my weapon. Here, at last, I had a chance of clearly seeing him. I had never set eyes on him before, so much was certain. He was small, as I have said; I was struck besides with the shocking expression of his face, with his remarkable combination of great muscular activity and great apparent debility of constitution, and – last but not least – with the odd, subjective disturbance caused by his neighbourhood. This bore some resemblance to incipient rigour, and was accompanied by a marked sinking of the pulse. At the time, I set it down to some idiosyncratic, personal distaste, and merely wondered at the acuteness of the symptoms; but I have since had reason to believe the cause to lie much deeper in the nature of man, and to turn on some nobler hinge than the principle of hatred.

This person (who had thus, from the first moment of his entrance, struck in me what I can only describe as a disgustful curiosity) was dressed in a fashion that would have made an ordinary person laughable. His clothes, that is to say, although they were of rich and sober fabric, were enormously too large for him in every measurement – the trousers hanging on his legs and rolled up to keep them from the ground, the waist of the coat below his haunches and the collar sprawling wide upon his shoulders. Strange to relate, this ludicrous accoutrement was far from moving me to laughter. Rather, as there was something abnormal and misbegotten in the very essence of the creature that now faced me – something seizing, surprising and revolting – this fresh disparity seemed but to fit in with and to reinforce it, so that to my interest in the man's nature and character there was added a curiosity as to his origin, his life, his fortune and status in the world.

These observations, though they have taken so great a space to be set down in, were yet the work of a few seconds. My visitor was, indeed, on fire with sombre excitement.

"Have you got it?" he cried. "Have you got it?" And so lively was his impatience that he even laid his hand upon my arm and sought to shake me.

I put him back, conscious at his touch of a certain icy pang along my blood. "Come, sir," said I. "You forget that I have not yet the pleasure of your acquaintance. Be seated, if you please." And I showed him an example, and sat down myself in my customary seat and with as fair an imitation of my ordinary manner to a patient, as the lateness of the hour, the nature of my preoccupations, and the horror I had of my visitor, would suffer me to muster.

"I beg your pardon, Dr Lanyon," he replied civilly enough. "What you say is very well founded and my impatience has shown its heels to my politeness. I come here at the instance of your colleague, Dr Henry Jekyll, on a piece of business of some moment, and I understood..." He paused and put his hand to his throat, and I could see, in spite of his collected manner, that he was wrestling against the approaches of the hysteria. " – I understood, a drawer..."

But here I took pity on my visitor's suspense, and some perhaps on my own growing curiosity.

"There it is, sir," said I, pointing to the drawer, where it lay on the floor behind a table and still covered with the sheet.

He sprang to it, and then paused, and laid his hand upon his heart – I could hear his teeth grate with the convulsive action of his jaws – and his face was so ghastly to see that I grew alarmed both for his life and reason.

"Compose yourself," said I.

He turned a dreadful smile to me, and as if with the decision of despair, plucked away the sheet. At sight of the contents, he uttered one loud sob of such immense relief that I sat petrified. And the next moment, in a voice that was already fairly well under control, "Have you a graduated glass?" he asked.

I rose from my place with something of an effort and gave him what he asked.

He thanked me with a smiling nod, measured out a few minims of the red tincture and added one of the powders. The mixture, which was at first of a reddish hue, began, in proportion as the crystals melted, to brighten in colour, to effervesce audibly, and to throw off small fumes of vapour. Suddenly and at the same moment, the boiling ceased and the compound changed to a dark purple, which faded again more slowly to a watery green. My visitor, who had watched these metamorphoses with a keen eye, smiled, set down the glass upon the table, and then turned and looked upon me with an air of scrutiny.

"And now," said he, "to settle what remains. Will you be wise? Will you be guided? Will you suffer me to take this glass in my hand and to go forth from your house without further parley? Or has the greed of curiosity too much command of you? Think before you answer, for it shall be done as you decide. As you decide, you shall be left as you were before, and neither richer nor wiser, unless the sense of service rendered to a man in mortal distress may be counted as a kind of riches of the soul. Or, if you shall so prefer to choose, a new province of knowledge and new avenues to fame and power shall be laid open to you, here, in this room, upon the instant; and your sight shall be blasted by a prodigy to stagger the unbelief of Satan."

"Sir," said I, affecting a coolness that I was far from truly possessing, "you speak enigmas, and you will perhaps not wonder that I hear you with no very strong impression of belief. But I have gone too far in the way of inexplicable services to pause before I see the end."

"It is well," replied my visitor. "Lanyon, you remember your vows: what follows is under the seal of our profession. And now, you who have so long been bound to the most narrow and material views, you who have denied the virtue of transcendental medicine, you who have derided your superiors – behold!"

He put the glass to his lips and drank at one gulp. A cry followed; he reeled, staggered, clutched at the table and held on, staring with injected eyes, gasping with open mouth; and as I looked there came, I thought, a change – he seemed to swell, his face became suddenly black and the features seemed to melt and alter – and the next moment, I had sprung to my feet and leapt back against the wall, my arm raised to shield me from that prodigy, my mind submerged in terror.

"O God!" I screamed, and "O God!" again and again; for there before my eyes – pale and shaken, and half-fainting, and groping before him with his hands, like a man restored from death – there stood Henry Jekyll!

What he told me in the next hour, I cannot bring my mind to set on paper. I saw what I saw, I heard what I heard, and my soul sickened at it – and yet now when that sight has faded from my eyes, I ask myself if I believe it and I cannot answer. My life is shaken to its roots. Sleep has left me; the deadliest terror sits by me at all hours; I feel that my days are numbered, and that I must die; and yet I shall die incredulous.

What Was It?

Fitz-James O'Brien
Extract

It was the tenth of July. After dinner was over I repaired with my friend, Dr Hammond, to the garden to smoke my evening pipe. The Doctor and myself found ourselves in an unusually metaphysical mood. We lit our large meerschaums, filled with fine Turkish tobacco; we paced to and fro, conversing. A strange perversity dominated the currents of our thought. They would *not* flow through the sunlit channels into which we strove to divert them. For some unaccountable reason they constantly diverged into dark and lonesome beds, where a continual gloom brooded. It was in vain that, after our old fashion, we flung ourselves on the shores of the East, and talked of its gay bazaars, of the splendours of the time of Haroun, of harems and golden palaces. Black genies continually arose from the depths of our talk, and expanded, like the one the fisherman released from the copper vessel, until they blotted everything bright from our vision. Insensibly, we yielded to the occult force that swayed us, and indulged in gloomy speculation. We had talked some time upon the proneness of the human mind to mysticism, and the almost universal love of the Terrible, when Hammond suddenly said to me, "What do you consider to be the greatest element of terror?"

The question, I own, puzzled me. That many things were terrible, I knew. Stumbling over a corpse in the dark; beholding, as I once did, a woman floating down a deep and rapid river, with wildly lifted arms and awful upturned face, uttering as she sank, shrieks that rent one's heart, while we, the spectators, stood frozen at a window which overhung the river at a height of sixty feet, unable to make the slightest effort to save her, but dumbly watching her last supreme agony and her disappearance. A shattered wreck, with no life visible, encountered floating listlessly on the ocean, is a terrible object, for it suggests a huge terror, the proportions of which are veiled. But it now struck me for the first time that there must be one great and ruling embodiment of fear – a 'king of terrors' to which all others must succumb. What might it be? To what train of circumstances would it owe its existence?

"I confess, Hammond," I replied to my friend, "I never considered the subject before. That there must be something more terrible than any other thing, I feel. I cannot attempt, however, even the most vague definition."

"I am somewhat like you, Harry," he answered. "I feel my capacity to experience a terror greater than anything yet conceived by the human mind – something combining in fearful and unnatural amalgamation hitherto supposed incompatible elements. The calling of the voices in Brockden Brown's novel of *Wieland* is awful; so is the picture of the Dweller of the Threshold, in Bulwer's *Zanoni*; but," he added, shaking his head gloomily, "there is something more horrible still than these."

"Look here, Hammond," I rejoined, "let us drop this kind of talk, for heaven's sake!"

"I don't know what's the matter with me tonight," he replied, "but my brain is running upon all sorts of weird and awful thoughts. I feel as if I could write a story like Hoffman tonight, if I were only master of a literary style."

"Well, if we are going to be Hoffmanesque in our talk, I'm off to bed. How sultry it is! Goodnight, Hammond."

"Goodnight, Harry. Pleasant dreams to you."

"To you, gloomy wretch, genies, ghouls, and enchanters."

We parted, and each sought his respective chamber. I undressed quickly and got into bed, taking with me, according to my usual custom, a book, over which I generally read myself to sleep. I opened the volume as soon as I had laid my head upon the pillow, and instantly flung it to the other side of the room. It was Goudon's *History of Monsters* – a curious French work which I had lately imported from Paris, but which, in the state of mind I had then reached, was anything but an agreeable companion. I resolved to go to sleep at once so, turning down my gas until nothing but a little blue point of light glimmered on the top of the tube, I composed myself to rest.

The room was in total darkness. The atom of gas that still remained lighted did not illuminate a distance of three inches round the burner. I desperately drew my arm across my eyes as if to shut out even the darkness, and tried to think of nothing. It was in vain. The confounded themes touched on by Hammond in the garden kept obtruding themselves on my brain. I battled against them. I erected ramparts of would-be blankness of intellect to keep them out. They still crowded upon me. While I was lying still as a corpse, hoping that by a perfect physical inaction I should hasten mental repose, an awful incident occurred. Something dropped, as it seemed, from the ceiling, plumb upon my chest, and I felt two bony hands encircling my throat, endeavouring to choke me.

I am no coward, and am possessed of considerable physical strength. The suddenness of the attack, instead of stunning me, strung every nerve to its highest tension. My body acted from instinct, before my brain had time to realize the terrors of my position. In an instant I wound two muscular arms around the creature and squeezed it, with all the strength of despair, against my chest. In a few seconds the bony hands that had fastened on my throat loosened their hold, and I was free to breathe once more. Then commenced a struggle of awful intensity. Immersed in the most profound darkness, totally ignorant of the nature of the thing by which I was so suddenly attacked, finding my grasp slipping every moment – by reason, it seemed to me, of the entire nakedness of my assailant – bitten with sharp teeth in the shoulder, neck and chest, having every moment to protect my throat against a pair of sinewy, agile hands, which my utmost efforts could not confine – these were a combination of circumstances to combat which required all the strength and skill and courage that I possessed.

At last, after a silent, deadly, exhausting struggle, I got my assailant under by a series of incredible efforts of strength. Once pinned, with my knee on what I made out to be its chest, I knew that I was victor. I rested for a moment to breathe. I heard the creature beneath me panting in the darkness, and felt the violent throbbing of a heart. It was apparently as exhausted as I was – that was one comfort. At this moment I remembered that I usually placed under my pillow, before going to bed, a large yellow silk pocket handkerchief, for use during the night. I felt for it instantly; it was there. In a few seconds more I had, after a fashion, pinioned the creature's arms.

I now felt tolerably secure. There was nothing more to be done but to turn on the gas and, having first seen what my midnight assailant was like, arouse the household. I will confess to being actuated by a certain pride in not giving the alarm before; I wished to make the capture alone and unaided.

Never losing my hold for an instant, I slipped from the bed to the floor, dragging my captive with me. I had but a few steps to make to reach the gas-burner and these I made with the greatest caution, holding the creature in a grip like a vice. At last I got within arm's length of the tiny speck of blue light which told me where the gas-burner lay. Quick as lightning I released my grasp with one hand and let on the full flood of light. Then I turned to look at my captive.

I cannot even attempt to give any definition of my sensations the instant after I turned on the gas. I suppose I must have shrieked with terror, for in less than a minute afterward my room was crowded with the inmates of the house. I shudder now as I think of that awful moment. *I saw nothing!* I had one arm firmly clasped round a breathing, panting, corporeal shape, my other hand gripped with all its strength a throat as warm, and apparently fleshly, as my own; and yet, with this living substance in my grasp, with its body pressed against my own, and all in the bright glare of a large jet of gas, I absolutely beheld nothing! Not even an outline – a vapour!

I do not, even at this hour, realize the situation in which I found myself. I cannot recall the astounding incident thoroughly. Imagination in vain tries to compass the awful paradox.

It breathed. I felt its warm breath upon my cheek. It struggled fiercely. It had hands. They clutched me. Its skin was smooth, like my own. There it lay, pressed close up against me, solid as stone – and yet utterly invisible!

I wonder that I did not faint or go mad on the instant. Some wonderful instinct must have sustained me; for, absolutely, in place of loosening my hold on the terrible Enigma, I seemed to gain an additional strength in my moment of horror, and tightened my grasp with such wonderful force that I felt the creature shivering with agony.

Just then Hammond entered my room at the head of the household. As soon as he beheld my face – which, I suppose, must have been an awful sight to look at – he hastened forward, crying, "Great heaven, Harry! What has happened?"

"Hammond! Hammond!" I cried, "Come here. Oh! This is awful! I have been attacked in bed by something or other, which I have hold of; but I can't see it – I can't see it!"

Hammond, doubtless struck by the unfeigned horror expressed in my countenance, made one or two steps forward with an anxious yet puzzled expression. A very audible titter burst from the remainder of my visitors.

"Harry," whispered Hammond, approaching me, "stop fooling about."

"I swear to you, Hammond, that this is no joke," I answered, in the same low tone. "Don't you see how it shakes my whole frame with its struggles? If you don't believe me, convince yourself. Feel it – touch it."

Hammond advanced and laid his hand on the spot I indicated. A wild cry of horror burst from him. He had felt it!

In a moment he had discovered somewhere in my room a long piece of cord, and was the next instant winding it and knotting it about the body of the unseen being that I clasped in my arms.

"Harry," he said, in a hoarse, agitated voice, for, though he preserved his presence of mind, he was deeply moved, "Harry, it's all safe now. You may let go, old fellow, if you're tired. The Thing can't move."

The confusion that ensued among the guests of the house who were witnesses of this extraordinary scene between Hammond and myself – who beheld the pantomime of binding this struggling something – who beheld me almost sinking from physical exhaustion when my task of jailer was over – the confusion and terror that took possession of the bystanders, when they saw all this, was beyond description. Still incredulity broke out through their terror. They had not the courage to satisfy themselves, and yet they doubted. They were incredulous. How could a solid, breathing body be invisible, they asked. My reply was this. I gave a sign to Hammond, and both of us lifted it from the ground, manacled as it was, and took it to my bed.

"Now, my friends," I said, as Hammond and myself held the creature suspended over the bed, "I can give you self-evident proof that here is a solid, ponderable body which, nevertheless, you cannot see. Be good enough to watch the surface of the bed attentively."

The eyes of the bystanders were immediately fixed on my bed. At a given signal Hammond and I let the creature fall. There was the dull sound of a heavy body alighting on a soft mass. The timbers of the bed creaked. A deep impression marked itself distinctly on the pillow, and on the bed itself. The crowd who witnessed this gave a low, universal cry and rushed from the room. Hammond and I were left alone.

We remained silent for some time, listening to the low, irregular breathing of the creature on the bed, and watching the rustle of the bedclothes as it impotently struggled to free itself from confinement. Then Hammond spoke.

"Harry, this is awful."

"Aye, awful."

"But not unaccountable."

"Not unaccountable! What do you mean? Such a thing has never occurred since the birth of the world!"

"Let us reason a little, Harry. Here is a solid body which we touch, but which we cannot see. The fact is so unusual that it strikes us with terror. Is there no parallel, though, for such a phenomenon? Take a piece of pure glass. It is tangible and transparent. A certain chemical coarseness is all that prevents its being so entirely transparent as to be totally invisible. It is not *theoretically impossible* to make a glass which shall not reflect a single ray of light – a glass so pure and homogeneous in its atoms that the rays from the sun shall pass through it. We do not see the air, and yet we feel it."

"That's all very well Hammond, but these are inanimate substances. Glass does not breathe, air does not breathe. *This* thing has a heart that palpitates – a will that moves it."

"You forget the strange phenomena of which we have so often heard of late," answered the Doctor, gravely. "At the meetings called 'spirit circles,' invisible hands have been thrust into the hands of those persons round the table – warm, fleshly hands that seemed to pulsate with mortal life."

What Was It?

"What? Do you think, then, that this thing is—"

"I don't know what it is," was the solemn reply.

We watched together, smoking many pipes, all night long, by the bedside of the unearthly being that tossed and panted until it was apparently wearied out. Then we learned by the low, regular breathing that it slept.

The next morning the house was all astir. The boarders congregated on the landing outside my room, and Hammond and myself were lions. We had to answer many questions as to the state of our strange prisoner, for as yet not one person except ourselves could be induced to set foot in the apartment.

The creature was awake. This was evidenced by the convulsive manner in which the bedclothes were moved in its efforts to escape.

Hammond and myself had racked our brains during the long night to discover some means by which we might realize the shape and general appearance of the Enigma. As well as we could make out by passing our hands over the creature's form, its outlines and lineaments were human. There was a mouth; a round, smooth head without hair; and a nose, which, however, was little elevated above the cheeks. At first we thought of placing the being on a smooth surface and tracing its outline with chalk, as shoemakers trace the outline of the foot. This plan was given up as being of no value. Such an outline would give not the slightest idea of its conformation.

A happy thought struck me. We would take a cast of it in

plaster of Paris. But how to do it? The movements of the creature would disturb the setting of the plastic covering, and distort the mould. Another thought: why not give it chloroform? It had respiratory organs – that was evident by its breathing. Once reduced to a state of insensibility, we could do with it what we would. Dr X— was sent for, and administered the chloroform. In three minutes after a well-known modeller of this city was busily engaged in covering the invisible form with the moist clay. In five minutes more we had a mould, and before evening a rough facsimile of the mystery. It was shaped like a man – distorted, but still a man. It was small, and its limbs revealed a muscular development that was unparalleled. Its face surpassed in hideousness anything I had ever seen. It was the physiognomy of what I should have fancied a ghoul to be. It looked as if it was capable of feeding on human flesh.

What was It?

Having satisfied our curiosity, and bound everyone in the house to secrecy, it became a question what was to be done with our enigma. It was impossible that we should keep such a horror in our house. It was equally impossible it should be let loose upon the world. Day after day this question was deliberated gravely.

The most singular part of the transaction was that we were entirely ignorant of what the creature habitually fed on. Everything in the way of nutriment that we could think of was placed before it, but was never touched. It was awful to stand by, day after day, and see the clothes toss, and hear the hard breathing, and know that it was starving.

Ten, twelve days, a fortnight passed, and it still lived. The pulsations of the heart, however, were daily growing fainter, and had now nearly ceased altogether. It was evident that the creature was dying for want of sustenance. I could not sleep of nights. Horrible as the creature was, it was pitiful to think of the pangs it was suffering.

At last it died. Hammond and I found it cold and stiff one morning in the bed. The heart had ceased to beat, the lungs to inspire. We hastened to bury it in the garden. It was a strange funeral, the dropping of that viewless corpse into the damp hole. The cast of its form I gave to Dr X—, who keeps it in his museum in Tenth Street.

FRANKENSTEIN

Mary Shelley

Extract

Darkness had no effect upon my fancy, and a churchyard was to me merely the receptacle of bodies deprived of life, which, from being the seat of beauty and strength, had become food for the worm. Now I was led to examine the cause and progress of this decay and forced to spend days and nights in vaults and charnel-houses. My attention was fixed upon every object the most insupportable to the delicacy of the human feelings. I saw how the fine form of man was degraded and wasted; I beheld the corruption of death succeed to the blooming cheek of life; I saw how the worm inherited the wonders of the eye and brain. I paused, examining and analysing all the minutiae of causation, as exemplified in the change from life to death, and death to life, until from the midst of this darkness a sudden light broke in upon me – a light so brilliant and wondrous, yet so simple, that while I became dizzy with the immensity of the prospect which it illustrated, I was surprised that among so many men of genius who had directed their inquiries towards the same science, that I alone should be reserved to discover so astonishing a secret.

It was on a dreary night of November that I beheld the accomplishment of my toils. With an anxiety that almost amounted to agony, I collected the instruments of life around me, that I might infuse a spark of being into the lifeless thing that lay at my feet. It was already one in the morning. The rain pattered dismally against the panes and my candle was nearly burnt out when, by the glimmer of the half-extinguished light, I saw the dull yellow eye of the creature open. It breathed hard, and a convulsive motion agitated its limbs.

How can I describe my emotions at this catastrophe, or how delineate the wretch whom with such infinite pains and care I had endeavoured to form? His limbs were in proportion, and I had selected his features as beautiful. Beautiful! Great God! His yellow skin scarcely covered the work of muscles and arteries beneath; his hair was of a lustrous black, and flowing; his teeth of a pearly whiteness; but these luxuriances only formed a more horrid contrast with his watery eyes, that seemed almost of the same colour as the dun white sockets in which they were set, his shrivelled complexion and straight black lips.

The different accidents of life are not so changeable as the feelings of human nature. I had worked hard for nearly two years, for the sole purpose of infusing life into an inanimate body. For this I had deprived myself of rest and health. I had desired it with an ardour that far exceeded moderation; but now that I had finished, the beauty of the dream vanished, and breathless horror and disgust filled my heart. Unable to endure the aspect of the being I had created, I rushed out of the room, and continued a long time traversing my bedchamber, unable to compose my mind to sleep.

At length lassitude succeeded to the tumult I had before endured; and I threw myself on the bed in my clothes, endeavouring to seek a few moments of forgetfulness. But it was in vain. I slept, indeed, but I was disturbed by the wildest dreams. I thought I saw Elizabeth, in the bloom of health, walking in the streets of Ingolstadt. Delighted and surprised, I embraced her; but as I imprinted the first kiss on her lips, they became livid with the hue of death; her features appeared to change, and I thought that I held the corpse of my dead mother in my arms; a shroud enveloped her form, and I saw the grave-worms crawling in the folds of the flannel.

I started from my sleep with horror. A cold dew covered my forehead, my teeth chattered, and every limb became convulsed: when, by the dim and yellow light of the moon, as it forced its way through the window shutters, I beheld the wretch – the miserable monster whom I had created. He held up the curtain of the bed; and his eyes, if eyes they may be called, were fixed on me. His jaws opened and he muttered some inarticulate sounds, while a grin wrinkled his cheeks. He might have spoken, but I did not hear. One hand was stretched out, seemingly to detain me – but I escaped and rushed downstairs. I took refuge in the courtyard belonging to the house which I inhabited; where I remained during the rest of the night, walking up and down in the greatest agitation, listening attentively, catching and fearing each sound as if it were to announce the approach of the demoniacal corpse to which I had so miserably given life. Oh! No mortal could support the horror of that countenance. A mummy again endued with animation could not be so hideous as that wretch. I had gazed on him while unfinished; he was ugly then, but when those muscles and joints were rendered capable of motion, it became a thing such as even Dante could not have conceived.

I passed the night wretchedly. Sometimes my pulse beat so quickly and hardly that I felt the palpitation of every artery; at others, I nearly sank to the ground through languor and extreme weakness. Mingled with this horror, I felt the bitterness of disappointment; dreams that had been my food and pleasant rest for so long a space were now become a hell to me; and the change was so rapid, the overthrow so complete!

The Story of Baelbrow

E and H Heron

It is a matter for regret that so many of Mr Flaxman Low's reminiscences should deal with the darker episodes of his experiences. Yet this is almost unavoidable, as the more purely scientific cases would not, perhaps, contain the same elements of interest for the general public, however valuable and instructive they might be to the expert student. It has also been considered better to choose the completer cases – those that ended in something like satisfactory proof – rather than the many instances where the thread broke off amongst surmisings, which it was never possible to subject to convincing tests.

The Story of Baelbrow

North of a low-lying strip of country on the East Anglian coast, the promontory of Bael Ness thrusts out a blunt nose into the sea. On the Ness, backed by pinewoods, stands a square, comfortable stone mansion, known to the countryside as Baelbrow. It has faced the east winds for close upon three hundred years, and during the whole period has been the home of the Swaffam family, who were never in anywise put out of conceit of their ancestral dwelling by the fact that it had always been haunted. Indeed, the Swaffams were proud of the Baelbrow Ghost, which enjoyed a wide notoriety, and no one dreamt of complaining of its behaviour until Professor Van der Voort of Louvain laid information against it, and sent an urgent appeal for help to Mr Flaxman Low.

The Professor, who was well acquainted with Mr Low, detailed the circumstances of his tenancy of Baelbrow, and the unpleasant events that had followed thereupon.

It appeared that Mr Swaffam, Senr., who spent a large portion of his time abroad, had offered to lend his house to the Professor for the summer season. When the Van der Voorts arrived at Baelbrow, they were charmed with the place. The prospect, though not very varied, was at least extensive, and the air exhilarating. Also the Professor's daughter enjoyed frequent visits from her betrothed – Harold Swaffam – and the Professor was delightfully employed in overhauling the Swaffam library.

The Van der Voorts had been duly told of the ghost, which lent distinction to the old house, but never in any way interfered with the comfort of the inmates. For some time they found this description to be strictly true, but with the beginning of October came a change. Up to this time and as far back as the Swaffam annals reached, the ghost had been a shadow, a rustle, a passing sigh – nothing definite or troublesome. But early in October strange things began to occur, and the terror culminated when a housemaid was found dead in a corridor three weeks later. Upon this the Professor felt that it was time to send for Flaxman Low.

Mr Low arrived upon a chilly evening when the house was already beginning to blur in the purple twilight, and the resinous scent of the pines came sweetly on the land breeze. Van der Voort welcomed him in the spacious, fire-lit hall. He was a stout man with a quantity of white hair, round eyes emphasized by spectacles, and a kindly, dreamy face. His life-study was philology, and his two relaxations: chess and the smoking of a big-bowled meerschaum.

"Now, Professor," said Mr Low when they had settled themselves in the smoking room. "How did it all begin?"

"I will tell you," replied Van der Voort, thrusting out his chin, and tapping his broad chest, and speaking as if an unwarrantable liberty had been taken with him. "First of all, it has shown itself to me!" Mr Flaxman Low smiled and assured him that nothing could be more satisfactory.

"But not at all satisfactory!" exclaimed the Professor. "I was sitting here alone, it might have been midnight, when I hear something come creeping like a little dog with its nails, *tick-tick*, upon the oak flooring of the hall. I whistle, for I think it is the little 'Rags' of my daughter, and afterwards opened the door, and I saw—' he hesitated and looked hard at Low through his spectacles, "something that was just disappearing into the passage which connects the two wings of the house. It was a figure, not unlike the human figure, but narrow and straight. I fancied I saw a bunch of black hair, and a flutter of something detached, which may have been a handkerchief. I was overcome by a feeling of repulsion. I heard a few clicking steps, then it stopped, as I thought, at the museum door. Come, I will show you the spot."

The Professor conducted Mr Low into the hall. The main staircase, dark and massive, yawned above them, and directly behind it ran the passage referred to by the Professor. It was over twenty feet long, and about midway led past a deep arch containing a door reached by two steps.

Van der Voort explained that this door formed the entrance to a large room called the museum, in which Mr Swaffam, Senr., who was something of a collector, stored the various curios he picked up during his excursions abroad. The Professor went on to say that he immediately followed the figure, which he believed had gone into the museum, but he found nothing there except the cases containing Swaffam's treasures.

"I mentioned my experience to no one. I concluded that I had seen the ghost. But two days after, one of the female servants coming through the passage, in the dark, declared that a man leapt out at her from the embrasure of the museum door, but she released herself and ran screaming into the servants' hall. We at once made a search but found nothing to substantiate her story.

"I took no notice of this, though it coincided pretty well with my own experience. The week after, my daughter Lena came down late one night for a book. As she was about to cross the hall, something leapt upon her from behind. Women are of little use in serious investigations – she fainted! Since then she has been ill and the doctor says 'run down'." Here the Professor spread out his hands. "So she leaves for a change tomorrow. Since then other members of the household have been attacked in much the same manner, with always the same result, they faint and are weak and useless when they recover.

"But, last Wednesday, the affair became a tragedy. By that time the servants had refused to come through the passage except in a crowd of three or four – most of them preferring to go round by the terrace to reach this part of the house. But one maid, named Eliza Freeman, said she was not afraid of the Baelbrow Ghost, and undertook to put out the lights in the hall one night. When she had done so, and was returning through the passage past the museum door, she appears to have been attacked, or at any rate frightened. In the grey of the morning they found her lying beside the steps, dead. There was a little blood upon her sleeve but no mark upon her body except a small raised pustule under the ear. The doctor said the girl was extraordinarily anaemic, and that she probably died from fright, her heart being weak. I was surprised at this, for she had always seemed to be a particularly strong and active young woman."

"Can I see Miss Van der Voort tomorrow before she goes?" asked Low, as the Professor signified he had nothing more to tell.

The Professor was rather unwilling that his daughter should be questioned, but he at last gave his permission, and next morning Low had a short talk with the girl before she left the house. He found her a very pretty girl, though listless and startlingly pale, and with a frightened stare in her light brown eyes. Mr Low asked if she could describe her assailant.

"No," she answered. "I could not see him for he was behind me. I only saw a dark, bony hand, with shining nails, and a bandaged arm pass just under my eyes before I fainted.'

"Bandaged arm? I have heard nothing of this."

"Tut-tut, mere fancy!" put in the Professor impatiently.

"I saw the bandages on the arm," repeated the girl, turning her head wearily away, "and I smelt the antiseptics it was dressed with."

"You have hurt your neck," remarked Mr Low, who noticed a small circular patch of pink under her ear.

She flushed and paled, raising her hand to her neck with a nervous jerk, as she said in a low voice: "It has almost killed me. Before he touched me, I knew he was there! I felt it!"

When they left her the Professor apologized for the unreliability of her evidence, and pointed out the discrepancy between her statement and his own.

"She says she sees nothing but an arm, yet I tell you it had no arms! Preposterous! Conceive a wounded man entering this house to frighten the young women! I do not know what to make of it! Is it a man, or is it the Baelbrow Ghost?"

During the afternoon when Mr Low and the Professor returned from a stroll on the shore, they found a dark-browed young man with a bull neck and strongly marked features standing sullenly before the hall fire. The Professor presented him to Mr Low as Harold Swaffam.

Swaffam seemed to be about thirty, but was already known as a far-seeing and successful member of the Stock Exchange.

"I am pleased to meet you, Mr Low," he began, with a keen glance, "though you don't look sufficiently high-strung for one of your profession."

Mr Low merely bowed.

"Come, you don't defend your craft against my insinuations?" went on Swaffam. "And so you have come to rout out our poor old ghost from Baelbrow? You forget that he is an heirloom, a family possession! What's this about his having turned rabid, eh, Professor?" he ended, wheeling round upon Van der Voort in his brusque way.

The Professor told the story over again. It was plain that he stood rather in awe of his prospective son-in-law.

"I heard much the same from Lena." said Swaffam. "It is my opinion that the women in this house are suffering from an epidemic of hysteria. You agree with me, Mr Low?"

"Possibly. Though hysteria could hardly account for Freeman's death."

"I can't say as to that until I have looked further into the particulars. I have not been idle since I arrived. I have examined the museum. No one has entered it from the outside, and there is no other way of entrance except through the passage. The flooring is laid, I happen to know, on a thick layer of concrete. And there the case for the ghost stands at present." After a few moments of dogged reflection, he swung round on Mr Low, in a manner that seemed peculiar to him when about to address any person. "What do you say to this plan, Mr Low? I propose to drive the Professor over to Ferryvale, to stop there for a day or two at the hotel, and I will also dispose of the servants who still remain in the house for, say, forty-eight hours. Meanwhile you and I can try to go further into the secret of the ghost's new pranks?"

Flaxman Low replied that this scheme exactly met his views, but the Professor protested against being sent away. Harold Swaffam, however, was a man who liked to arrange things in his own fashion, and within forty-five minutes he and Van der Voort departed in the dogcart.

The evening was lowering, and Baelbrow, like all houses built in exposed situations, was extremely susceptible to the changes of the weather. Therefore, before many hours were over, the place was full of creaking noises as the screaming gale battered at the shuttered windows, and the tree branches tapped and groaned against the walls.

Harold Swaffam on his way back was caught in the storm and drenched to the skin. It was therefore settled that after he had changed his clothes he should have a couple of hours' rest on the smoking-room sofa, while Mr Low kept watch in the hall.

The early part of the night passed over uneventfully. A light burned faintly in the great wainscotted hall, but the passage was dark. There was nothing to be heard but the wild moan and whistle of the wind coming in from the sea, and the squalls of rain dashing against the windows.

As the hours advanced, Mr Low lit a lantern that lay at hand and, carrying it along the passage, tried the museum door. It yielded, and the wind came muttering through to meet him. He looked round at the shutters and behind the big cases which held Mr Swaffam's treasures, to make sure that the room contained no living occupant but himself.

Suddenly he fancied he heard a scraping noise behind him, and turned round, but discovered nothing to account for it. Finally, he laid the lantern on a bench so that its light should fall through the door into the passage, and returned again to the hall, where he put out the lamp, and then once more took up his station by the closed door of the smoking room.

A long hour passed, during which the wind continued to roar down the wide hall chimney, and the old boards creaked as if furtive footsteps were gathering from every corner of the house. But Flaxman Low heeded none of these; he was awaiting for a certain sound.

After a while, he heard it – the cautious scraping of wood on wood. He leant forward to watch the museum door. *Click, click*, came the curious dog-like tread upon the tiled floor of the museum, till the thing, whatever it was, paused and listened behind the open door. The wind lulled at the moment, and Low listened also, but no further sound was to be heard, only slowly across the broad ray of light falling through the door grew a stealthy shadow.

Again the wind rose, and blew in heavy gusts about the house, till even the flame in the lantern flickered; but when it steadied once more, Flaxman Low saw that the silent form had passed through the door, and was now on the steps outside. He could just make out a dim shadow in the dark angle of the embrasure.

Presently, from the shapeless shadow came a sound Mr Low was not prepared to hear. The thing sniffed the air with the strong, audible inspiration of a bear, or some large animal. At the same moment, carried on the draughts of the hall, a faint, unfamiliar odour reached his nostrils. Lena Van der Voort's words flashed back upon him – this, then, was the creature with the bandaged arm!

Again, as the storm shrieked and shook the windows, a darkness passed across the light. The thing had sprung out from the angle of the door, and Flaxman Low knew that it was making its way towards him through the illusive blackness of the hall. He hesitated for a second; then he opened the smoking-room door that creaked as he opened it.

Harold Swaffam sat up on the sofa, dazed with sleep. "What has happened? Has it come?"

Low told him what he had just seen. Swaffam listened half-smilingly.

"What do you make of it now?" he said.

"I must ask you to defer that question for a little," replied Low.

"Then you mean me to suppose that you have a theory to fit all these incongruous items?"

"I have a theory, which may be modified by further knowledge," said Low. "Meantime, am I right in concluding from the name of this house that it was built on a barrow or burying-place?'

"You are right, though that has nothing to do with the latest freaks of our ghost," returned Swaffam decidedly.

"I also gather that Mr Swaffam has lately sent home one of the many cases now lying in the museum?" went on Mr Low.

"He sent one, certainly, last September."

"And you have opened it," asserted Low.

"Yes – though I flattered myself I had left no trace of my handiwork."

"I have not examined the cases," said Low. "I inferred that you had done so from other facts."

"Now, one thing more," went on Swaffam, still smiling. "Do you imagine there is any danger – I mean to men like ourselves? Hysterical women cannot be taken into serious account.”

“Certainly; the gravest danger to any person who moves about this part of the house alone after dark,” replied Low.

Harold Swaffam leant back and crossed his legs.

“To go back to the beginning of our conversation, Mr Low, may I remind you of the various conflicting particulars you will have to reconcile before you can present any decent theory to the world?”

“I am quite aware of that.”

“First of all, our original ghost was a mere misty presence, rather guessed at from vague sounds and shadows – now we have a something that is tangible, and that can, as we have proof, kill with fright. Next Van der Voort declares the thing was a narrow, long and distinctly armless object, while Miss Van der Voort has not only seen the arm and hand of a human being, but saw them clearly enough to tell us that the nails were gleaming and the arm bandaged. She also felt its strength. Van der Voort, on the other hand, maintained that it clicked along like a dog – you bear out this description with the additional information that it sniffs like a wild beast. Now what can this thing be? It is capable of being seen, smelt and felt, yet it hides itself successfully in a room where there is no cavity or space sufficient to afford covert to a cat! You still tell me that you believe that you can explain this phenomenon?’

"Most certainly," replied Flaxman Low with conviction.

"I have not the slightest intention or desire to be rude, but as a mere matter of common sense, I must express my opinion plainly. I believe the whole thing to be the result of excited imaginations, and I am about to prove it. Do you think there is any further danger tonight?"

"Very great danger tonight," replied Low.

"Very well. As I said, I am going to prove it. I will ask you to allow me to lock you up in one of the distant rooms, where I can get no help from you, and I will pass the remainder of the night walking about the passage and hall in the dark."

"You can do so if you wish, but I must at least beg to be allowed to look on. I will leave the house and watch what goes on from the window in the passage, which I saw opposite the museum door. You cannot, in any fairness, refuse to let me be a witness."

"I cannot, of course," returned Swaffam. "Still, the night is too bad to turn a dog out into, and I warn you that I shall lock you out."

"That will not matter. Lend me a macintosh, and leave the lantern lit in the museum, where I placed it."

Swaffam agreed to this.

Mr Low gives a graphic account of what followed. He left the house and was duly locked out, and, after groping his way round the house, found himself at length outside the window of the passage, which was almost opposite to the door of the museum. The door was still ajar and a thin band of light cut out into the gloom. Further down the hall gaped black and void. Low, sheltering himself as well as he could from the rain, waited for Swaffam 's appearance. Was the terrible yellow watcher balancing itself upon its lean legs in the dim corner opposite, ready to spring out with its deadly strength upon the passer-by?

Presently Low heard a door bang inside the house, and the next moment Swaffam appeared with a candle in his hand, an isolated spread of weak rays against the vast darkness behind. He advanced steadily down the passage, his dark face grim and set, and as he came Mr Low experienced that tingling sensation, which is so often the forerunner of some strange experience.

Swaffam passed on towards the other end of the passage. There was a quick vibration of the museum door as a lean shape with a shrunken head leapt out into the passage after him. Then all together came a hoarse shout, the noise of a fall and utter darkness.

In an instant, Mr Low had broken the glass, opened the window, and swung himself into the passage. There he lit a match and as it flared he saw by its dim light a picture painted for a second upon the obscurity beyond.

Swaffam's big figure lay with outstretched arms, face downwards, and as Low looked a crouching shape extricated itself from the fallen man, raising a narrow vicious head from his shoulder.

The match spluttered feebly and went out, and Low heard a flying step click on the boards, before he could find the candle

Swaffam had dropped. Lighting it, he stooped over Swaffam and turned him on his back. The man's strong colour had gone, and the wax-white face looked whiter still against the blackness of hair and brows. And upon his neck under the ear was a little raised pustule, from which a thin line of blood was streaked up to the angle of his cheekbone.

Some instinctive feeling prompted Low to glance up at this moment. Half extended from the museum doorway were a face and bony neck – a high-nosed, dull-eyed, malignant face, the eye sockets hollow, and the darkened teeth showing. Low plunged his hand into his pocket and a shot rang out in the echoing passageway and hall. The wind sighed through the broken panes, a ribbon of stuff fluttered along the polished flooring, and that was all, as Flaxman Low half dragged, half carried Swaffam into the smoking room.

It was some time before Swaffam recovered consciousness. He listened to Low's story of how he had found him with a red angry gleam in his sombre eyes.

"The ghost has scored off me," he said, with an odd, sullen laugh, "but now I fancy it's my turn! But before we adjourn to the museum to examine the place, I will ask you to let me hear your notion of things. You have been right in saying there was real danger. For myself I can only tell you that I felt something spring upon me, and I knew no more. Had this not happened I am afraid I should never have asked you a second time what your idea of the matter might be," he added.

"There are two main indications," replied Low. "This strip of yellow bandage, which I have just now picked up from the passage floor, and the mark on your neck."

"What's that you say?" Swaffam rose quickly and examined his neck in a small glass beside the mantelshelf.

"Connect those two, and I think I can leave you to work it out for yourself," said Low.

"Pray let us have your theory in full," requested Swaffam shortly.

"Very well," answered Low good-humouredly – he thought Swaffam's annoyance natural in the circumstances. The long, narrow figure that seemed to the Professor to be armless is developed on the next occasion. For Miss Van der Voort sees a bandaged arm and a dark hand with gleaming – which means gilded – nails. The clicking sound of the footsteps coincides with these particulars, for we know that sandals made of strips of leather are not uncommon in company with gilt nails and bandages. Old and dry leather would naturally click upon your polished floor."

"Bravo, Mr Low! So you mean to say that this house is haunted by a mummy!"

"All that I have seen confirms this idea."

"To do you justice, you held

this theory before to-night – before, in fact, you had seen anything for yourself. You gathered that my father had sent home a mummy, and you went on to conclude that I had opened the case?"

"Yes. I imagine you took off most of – or rather all – the outer bandages, thus leaving the limbs free, wrapped only in the inner bandages which were swathed round each separate limb. I fancy this mummy was preserved on the Theban method with aromatic spices, which left the skin olive-coloured, dry and flexible, like tanned leather, the features remaining distinct, and the hair, teeth and eyebrows perfect."

"So far, good," said Swaffam. "But now, how about the intermittent vitality? The pustule of blood on the neck of those whom it attacks? And where is our old friend the Baelbrow ghost to come in?"

Swaffam tried to speak in a rallying tone, but his excitement and lowering temper were visible enough, in spite of the attempts he made to suppress them.

"To begin at the beginning," said Flaxman Low, "everybody who, in a rational and honest manner, investigates the phenomena of spiritism will, sooner or later, meet in them some perplexing element, which is not to be explained by any of the ordinary theories. For reasons into which I need not now enter, this present case appears to me to be one of these. I am led to believe that the ghost which has for so many years given dim and vague manifestations of its existence in this house is, in fact, a vampire."

Swaffam threw back his head with an incredulous gesture.

"We no longer live in the middle ages, Mr Low! And besides, how could a vampire come here?" he said scoffingly.

"It is held by some authorities on these subjects that under certain conditions a vampire may be self-created. You tell me that this house is built upon an ancient barrow, in fact, on a spot where we might naturally expect to find such an elemental psychic germ. In those dead human systems were contained all the seeds for good and evil. The power which causes these psychic seeds or germs to grow is thought, and from being long dwelt on and indulged, a thought might finally gain a mysterious vitality, which could go on increasing more and more by attracting to itself suitable and appropriate elements from its environment. For a long period this germ remained a helpless intelligence, awaiting the opportunity to assume some material form, by means of which to carry out its desires. Now, we can only judge of the nature of the germ by its manifestation through matter. Here we have every indication of a vampire intelligence touching into life and energy the dead human frame. Hence the mark on the neck of its victims, and their bloodless and anaemic condition. For a vampire, as you know, sucks blood."

"Now, for proof," said Swaffam. "Wait a second, Mr Low. You say you fired at this appearance?" And he took up the pistol which Low had laid down on the table.

"Yes, I aimed at a small portion of its foot which I saw on the step."

Without more words, and with the pistol still in his hand, Swaffam led the way to the Museum.

The wind howled round the house, and darkness lay upon the world, when the two men looked upon one of the strangest sights it has ever been given to men to shudder at.

Half in and half out of an oblong wooden box in a corner of the great room, lay a lean shape in its rotten yellow bandages, the scraggy neck surmounted by a mop of frizzled hair. The toe strap of a sandal and a portion of the left foot had been shot away.

Swaffam, with a working face, gazed down at it, then seizing it by its tearing bandages, he flung it into the box, where it fell into a lifelike posture, its wide, moist-lipped mouth gaping up at them.

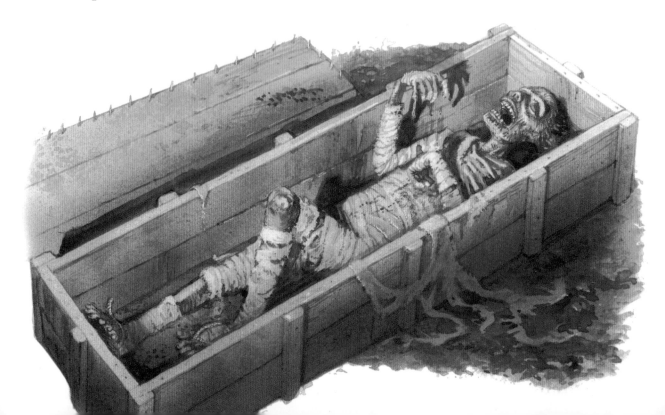

For a moment Swaffam stood over the thing; then with a curse he raised the revolver and shot into the grinning face again and again with a deliberate vindictiveness. Finally he rammed the thing down into the box, and, clubbing the weapon, smashed the head into fragments with a vicious energy that coloured the whole horrible scene with a suggestion of murder done.

Then, turning to Low, he said "Help me to fasten the cover on it."

"Are you going to bury it?"

"No, we must rid the earth of it," he answered savagely. "I'll put it into the old canoe and burn it."

The rain had ceased when in the daybreak they carried the old canoe down to the shore. In it they placed the mummy case with its ghastly occupant. The sail was raised and the vessel set alight, and Low and Swaffam watched it drift away, at first a tiny spark, then a flare and waving fire – until far out to sea the history of that dead thing ended three thousand years after the priests of Armen had laid it to rest in its appointed pyramid.

DRacula

Bram Stoker

Extract

I was awakened by the Count, who looked at me as grimly as a man could look as he said, "Tomorrow, my friend, we must part. You return to your beautiful England, I to some work which may have such an end that we may never meet. Your letter home has been despatched. Tomorrow I shall not be here, but all shall be ready for your journey. In the morning come the Szgany, who have some labours of their own here, and also come some Slovaks. When they have gone, my carriage shall come for you, and shall bear you to the Borgo Pass to meet the diligence from Bukovina to Bistritz. But I am in hopes that I shall see more of you at Castle Dracula."

I suspected him, and determined to test his sincerity. Sincerity! It seems like a profanation of the word to write it in connection with such a monster, so I asked him point-blank, "Why may I not go tonight?"

"Because, dear sir, my coachman and horses are away on a mission."

"But I would walk with pleasure. I want to get away at once."

He smiled, such a soft, smooth, diabolical smile that I knew there was some trick behind it. He said, "And your baggage?"

"I do not care about it. I can send for it some other time."

The Count stood up, and said, with a sweet courtesy which made me rub my eyes, it seemed so real, "You English have a saying which is close to my heart, for its spirit is that which rules our *boyars*, 'Welcome the coming, speed the parting guest.' Come with me, my dear young friend. Not an hour shall you wait in my house against your will, though sad am I at your going, and that you so suddenly desire it. Come!" With a stately gravity, he, with the lamp, preceded me down the stairs and along the hall. Suddenly he stopped. "Hark!"

Close at hand came the howling of many wolves. It was almost as if the sound sprang up at the rising of his hand, just as the music of a great orchestra seems to leap under the baton of the conductor. After a pause of a moment, he proceeded, in his stately way, to the door, drew back the ponderous bolts, unhooked the heavy chains, and began to draw it open.

To my astonishment I saw that it was unlocked. Suspiciously, I looked all round, but could see no key of any kind.

As the door began to open, the howling of the wolves

outside grew louder and angrier. Their red jaws, with champing teeth, and their blunt-clawed feet as they leapt, came in through the opening door. I knew then that to struggle at the moment against the Count was useless. With such allies as these at his command, I could do nothing.

But still the door continued slowly to open, and only the Count's body stood in the gap. Suddenly it struck me that this might be the moment and means of my doom. I was to be given to the wolves, and at my own instigation. There was a diabolical wickedness in the idea great enough for the Count, and as the last chance I cried out, "Shut the door! I shall wait till morning." And I covered my face with my hands to hide my tears of disappointment.

With one sweep of his powerful arm the Count threw the door shut, and the great bolts clanged and echoed through the hall.

In silence we returned to the library, and after a minute or two I went to my own room. The last I saw of Count Dracula was his kissing his hand to me, with a red light of triumph in his eyes and a smile that Judas in hell might be proud of.

When I was in my room and about to lie down, I thought I heard a whispering at my door. I went to it softly and listened. Unless my ears deceived me, I heard the voice of the Count.

"Back to your own place! Your time is not yet come. Wait! Have patience! Tonight is mine. Tomorrow night is yours!"

There was a low, sweet ripple of laughter, and in a rage I threw open the door, and saw beyond the three terrible women licking their lips. As I appeared, they all joined in a horrible laugh, and ran away.

I came back to my room and threw myself on my knees. It is then so near the end? Tomorrow! Lord, help me!

I slept till just before the dawn, and when I woke threw myself on my knees, for I determined that if Death came he should find me ready.

At last I felt that subtle change in the air, and knew that the morning had come. Then came the welcome cock crow, and I felt that I was safe. With a glad heart, I opened the door and ran down the hall. I had seen that the door was unlocked, and now escape was before me. With hands that trembled with eagerness, I unhooked the chains and threw back the massive bolts.

But the door would not move. Despair seized me. I pulled and pulled at the door, and shook it till, massive as it was, it rattled in its casement. I could see the bolt shot. It had been locked after I left the Count.

Then a wild desire took me to obtain the key at any risk, and I determined then and there to scale the wall again, and gain the Count's room. He might kill me, but death now seemed the happier choice of evils. Without a pause I rushed up to the east window, and scrambled down the wall as before, into the Count's room. It was empty, but that was as I expected. I could not see a key anywhere, but the heap of gold remained. I went through the door in the corner and down the winding stair and along the dark passage to the old chapel. I knew now well enough where to find the monster I sought.

The great box was in the same place, close against the wall, but the lid was laid on it, not fastened down, but with the nails ready in their places to be hammered home.

I knew I must search the body for the key, so I raised the lid, and laid it back against the wall. And then I saw something which filled my very soul with horror. There lay the Count, but looking as if his youth had been half restored. For the white hair and moustache were changed to dark iron-grey. The cheeks were fuller, and the white skin seemed ruby-red underneath. The mouth was redder than ever, for on the lips were gouts of fresh blood, which trickled from the corners of the mouth and ran down over the chin and neck. Even the deep, burning eyes seemed set amongst swollen flesh, for the lids and pouches underneath were bloated. It seemed as if the whole awful creature were simply gorged with blood. He lay like a filthy leech, exhausted with his repletion.

I shuddered as I bent over to touch him and every sense in me revolted at the contact – but I had to search, or I was lost. The coming night might see my own body a banquet in a similar way to those horrid three. I felt all over the body, but no sign could I find of the key. Then I stopped and looked at the Count. There was a mocking smile on the bloated face which seemed to drive me mad. This was the being I was helping to transfer to London, where, perhaps, for centuries to come he might, amongst its teeming millions, satiate his lust for blood, and create a new and ever-widening circle of semi-demons to batten on the helpless.

The very thought drove me mad. A terrible desire came upon me to rid the world of such a monster. There was no lethal weapon at hand, but I seized a shovel that the workmen had been using to fill the cases, and lifting it high, struck, with the edge downward, at the hateful face. But as I did so the head turned, and the eyes fell upon me, with all their blaze of basilisk horror. The sight seemed to paralyze me, and the shovel turned in my hand and glanced from the face, merely making a deep gash above the forehead. The shovel fell from my hand across the box, and as I pulled it away the flange of the blade caught the edge of the lid, which fell over again, and hid the horrid thing from my sight. The last glimpse I had was of the bloated face, bloodstained and fixed with a grin of malice which would have held its own in the nethermost hell.

I thought and thought what should be my next move, but my brain seemed on fire, and I waited with a despairing feeling growing over me. As I waited I heard in the distance a gipsy song sung by merry voices coming closer, and through their song the rolling of heavy wheels and the cracking of whips. The Szgany and the Slovaks of whom the Count had spoken were coming. With a last look around and at the box that contained the vile body, I ran from the place and gained the Count's room, determined to rush out at the moment the door should be opened. With strained ears I listened, and heard downstairs the grinding of the key in the great lock and the falling back of the heavy door. There must have been some other means of entry, or someone had a key for one of the locked doors.

Then there came the sound of many feet tramping and dying away in some passage which sent up a clanging echo. I turned to run down again towards the vault, where I might find the new entrance, but at the moment there seemed to come a violent puff of wind, and the door to the winding stair blew to with a shock that set the dust from the lintels flying. When I ran to push it open, I found that it was hopelessly fast. I was again a prisoner, and the net of doom was closing round me.

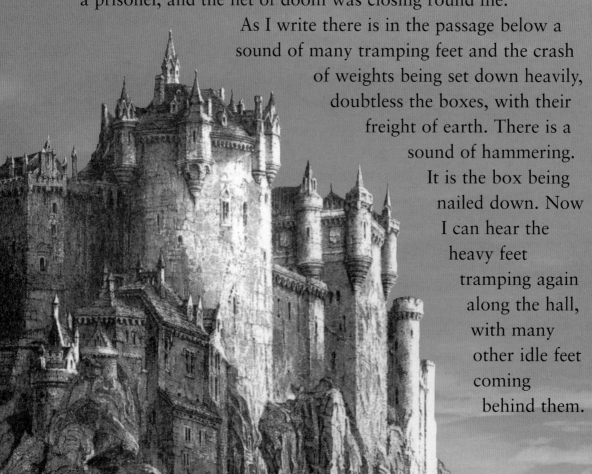

As I write there is in the passage below a sound of many tramping feet and the crash of weights being set down heavily, doubtless the boxes, with their freight of earth. There is a sound of hammering. It is the box being nailed down. Now I can hear the heavy feet tramping again along the hall, with many other idle feet coming behind them.

The door is shut; the chains rattle. There is a grinding of the key in the lock. I can hear the key withdrawn, then another door opens and shuts. I hear the creaking of lock and bolt.

Hark! In the courtyard and down the rocky way the roll of heavy wheels, the crack of whips, and the chorus of the Szgany as they pass into the distance.

I am alone in the castle with those horrible women. Faugh! Mina is a woman, and there is nought in common. They are devils of the Pit!

I shall not remain alone with them. I shall try to scale the castle wall farther than I have yet attempted. I may find a way from this dreadful place.

And then away for home! Away to the quickest and nearest train! Away from the cursed spot, from this cursed land, where the devil and his children still walk with earthly feet!

At least God's mercy is better than that of those monsters, and the precipice is steep and high. At its foot a man may sleep – as a man. Goodbye, all Mina!

Man-size in Marble

E Nesbit

Although every word of this story is as true as despair, I do not expect people to believe it. Nowadays a 'rational explanation' is required before belief is possible. Let me then, at once, offer the 'rational explanation' which finds most favour among those who have heard the tale of my life's tragedy. It is held that we were 'under a delusion,' Laura and I, on that 31st of October; and that this supposition places the whole matter on a satisfactory and believable basis. The reader can judge, when he, too, has heard my story, how far this is an 'explanation,' and in what sense it is 'rational.' There were three who took part in this; Laura and I and another man. The other man still lives, and can speak to the truth of the least credible part of my story.

I never knew in my life what it was to have as much money as I required to supply the most ordinary needs of life: good colours, canvases, brushes, books and cab-fares and when we were married, we knew quite well that we should only be able to live at all by 'strict punctuality and attention to business.' I used to paint in those days, and Laura used to write, and we felt sure we could keep the pot at least simmering. Living in town was out of the question, so we went to look for a cottage in the country, which should be at once sanitary and picturesque. So rarely do these two qualities meet in one cottage that our search was for some time quite fruitless. We tried advertisements, but most of the desirable rural residences which we did look at, proved to be lacking in both essentials; and when a cottage chanced to have drains, it always had stucco as well and was shaped like a tea-caddy. And if we found a vine or rose-covered porch, corruption invariably lurked within. Our minds got so befogged by the eloquence of estate agents, and the rival disadvantages of the fever-traps and outrages to beauty which we had seen and scorned, that I very much doubt whether either of us on our wedding morning, knew the difference between a house and a haystack. But when we got away from friends and estate agents, on our honeymoon, our wits grew clear again, and we knew a pretty cottage when at last we saw one.

It was at Brenzett, a little village set on a hill over against the southern marshes. We had gone there, from the seaside village where we were staying, to see the church, and two fields from the church we found this cottage. It stood quite by itself, about two miles from the village. It was a low building, with rooms sticking out in unexpected places. There was a bit of stonework – moss-grown – just two old rooms, all that was left of a big house that had once stood there; and round this stone-work the house had grown up. It was charming, and after a brief examination we took it. It was absurdly cheap.

The rest of our honeymoon we spent in grubbing about in second-hand shops in the county town, picking up bits of old oak and Chippendale chairs for our furnishing. We wound up with a run up to town and a visit to Liberty's, and soon the low oak-beamed lattice-windowed rooms began to be home. There was a jolly old-fashioned garden at the back, with grass paths, and no end of hollyhocks and sunflowers, and big lilies. From the window you could see the marsh pastures, and beyond them the beautiful blue, thin line of the sea.

We were as happy as the summer was glorious, and settled down into work sooner than we ourselves expected. I was never tired of sketching the view and the wonderful cloud effects from the open lattice, and Laura would sit at the table and write verses about them, in which I mostly played the part of foreground.

We got a tall old peasant woman to housekeep for us. Her face and figure were good, though her cooking was of the homeliest; but she understood all about gardening, and told us all the old names of the coppices and cornfields, and the stories of the smugglers and highwaymen, and, better still, of the 'things that walked,' and of the 'sights' which met one in lonely glens of a starlight night. She was a great comfort to us, because Laura hated housekeeping as much as I loved folklore, and we soon came to leave all the domestic business to Mrs Dorman, and to use her legends in little magazine stories which brought in the jingling guinea.

We had three months of married happiness, and did not have a single quarrel. One October evening I had been down to smoke a pipe with the doctor – our only neighbour – a pleasant young Irishman. Laura had stayed at home to finish a comic sketch of a village episode for the *Monthly Marplot*. I left her laughing over her own jokes, and came in to find her a crumpled heap of pale muslin weeping on the window seat.

"Good heavens, my darling, what's the matter?" I cried, taking her in my arms. She leaned her little dark head against my shoulder and went on crying. I had never seen her cry before – we had always been so happy, you see – and I felt sure some frightful misfortune had happened.

"What *is* the matter? Do speak."

"It's Mrs Dorman," she sobbed.

"What has she done?" I inquired, immensely relieved that it was not a serious matter.

"She says she must go before the end of the month, that her niece is ill – she's gone down to see her now – tonight. But I don't believe that's the real, true reason, because her niece is always ill. I believe someone in the village may have been been setting her against us. Her manner was so very peculiar – she was not at all like her usual self."

"Never mind darling," I said. "Whatever you do, don't cry, or I shall have to cry too, to keep you in countenance, and then you'll never respect your man again!"

She dried her eyes obediently on my handkerchief, and even tried to smile, though it was a faint version of her usual pretty one. "But you see," she went on, "it is really serious, because these village people are so sheepy, and if one won't do a thing you may be quite sure none of the others will. And I shall have to cook the dinners, and wash up the hateful greasy plates; and you'll have to carry cans of water about, and clean the boots and knives and we shall never have any time for work, or to earn any money, or anything. We shall have to work hard all day, and only be able to have a slight respite when we are waiting for the kettle to boil!"

I represented to her that even if we had to perform these duties, the day would still present some margin for other toils and recreations. But would not see the matter in any but the greyest light. She was very unreasonable but I could not have loved her more if she had been as reasonable as Whately.

Man-Size in Marble

"I'll speak to Mrs Dorman when she comes back, and see if I can't come to terms with her," I said. "Perhaps she only wants a rise in her pay. I am sure it will be all right. Let's walk up to the church together."

The church was a large and lonely one, and we loved to go there, especially upon bright nights. The path skirted a wood, cut through it once, and ran along the crest of the hill through two meadows, and round the churchyard wall, over which the old yews loomed in black masses of shadow. This path, which was partly paved, was called 'the bier-balk,' for it had long been the way by which the corpses had been carried to burial. The churchyard was richly treed, and was shaded by great elms which stood just outside and stretched their majestic arms in benediction over the happy dead. A large, low porch let one into the building by a Norman doorway and a heavy oak door studded with iron.

Inside, the arches rose into darkness, and between them the reticulated windows, which stood out white in the moonlight. In the chancel, the windows were of rich glass, which showed in faint light their noble colouring, and made the black oak of the choir pews hardly more solid than the shadows. But on each side of the altar lay a grey marble figure of a knight in full plate armour lying upon a low slab, with hands held up in everlasting prayer. And these figures, oddly enough, were always to be seen if there was even the slightest glimmer of light in the church.

Their names were lost, but the peasants told of them that

they had been fierce and wicked men, marauders by land and sea, who had been the scourge of their time, and had been guilty of deeds so foul that the house they had lived in – the big house, by the way, that had stood on the site of our cottage – had been stricken by lightning and the vengeance of heaven. But for all that, the gold of their heirs had bought them a place in the church. Looking at the bad, hard faces reproduced in the marble, this story was easily believed.

The church looked at its best and weirdest on that night, for the shadows of the yew trees fell through the windows upon the

floor of the nave and touched the pillars with tattered shade. We sat down together without speaking, and watched the solemn beauty of the old church, with some of that awe which inspired its early builders. We walked to the chancel and looked at the sleeping warriors. Then we rested some time on the stone seat in the porch, looking out over the stretch of quiet moonlit meadows, feeling in every fibre of our being the peace of the night and of our happy love; and came away at last with a sense that even scrubbing and blackleading were but small troubles at their worst.

Mrs Dorman had come back from the village, and I at once invited her to a *tête-à-tête*. "Now, Mrs Dorman," I said, when I had got her into my painting room, "what's all this about your not staying with us?"

"I should be glad to get away, sir, before the end of the month," she answered, with her usual placid dignity.

"Have you any fault to find, Mrs Dorman?"

"None at all, sir. You and your lady have always been most kind, I'm sure—"

"Well, what is it? Are your wages not high enough?"

"No, sir, I gets quite enough."

"Then why not stay?"

"I'd rather not," she said with some hesitation, "my niece is very ill."

"But your niece has been ill ever since we came."

No answer. There was a long and awkward silence.

Eventually I broke it.

"Can't you stay for another month?" I asked.

"No, sir. I'm bound to go by Thursday."

And this was Monday!

"Well, I must say, I think you might have let us know before. There's no time now to get anyone else, and your mistress is not fit to do heavy housework. Can't you stay till next week?"

"I might be able to come back next week."

I was now convinced that all she wanted was a brief holiday, which we should have been willing enough to let her have, as soon as we could get a substitute.

"But why must you go this week?" I persisted. "Come, out with it."

Mrs Dorman drew the little shawl, which she always wore, tightly across her bosom, as though she were cold. Then she said, with a sort of effort: "They say, sir, as this was a big house in Catholic times, and there was a many deeds done here."

The nature of the 'deeds' might be vaguely inferred from the inflection of Mrs Dorman's voice which was enough to make one's blood run cold. I was glad that Laura was not in the room. She was always nervous, as highly-strung natures are, and I felt that these tales about our house might have made our home less dear to my wife.

"Tell me all about it, Mrs Dorman," I said "You needn't mind about telling me. I'm not like the young people who make fun of such things."

Which was partly true.

"Well, sir," she sank her voice, "you may have seen in the church, beside the altar, two shapes."

"You mean the effigies of the knights in armour," I said cheerfully.

"I mean them two bodies, drawed out man-size in marble," she returned, and I had to admit that her description was a thousand times more graphic than mine'.

"They do say, as on All Saints' Eve them two bodies sits up on their slabs, and gets off of them, and then walks down the aisle, *in their marble* and as the church clock strikes eleven they walks out of the church door, and along the bier-balk, and if it's wet there'll be footprints left in the morning."

"And where do they go?" I asked.

"They comes back here to their home, sir, and if anyone meets them—"

"Well, what then?" I asked.

But she only repeated that her niece was ill and she must go. I scorned to discuss the niece, and tried to get from Mrs Dorman more details of the legend. I could get nothing but warnings.

"Whatever you do, sir, lock the door early on All Saints' Eve, and make the cross sign over the doorstep and on the windows."

"But is their evidence that anyone has ever seen these dreadful things?" I persisted.

"That's not for me to say. I know what I know, sir."

"Well, who was here last year?"

"No one, sir. The lady as owned the house only stayed here in summer, and she always went to London a full month afore *the* night. And I'm sorry to inconvenience you and your lady, but my niece is ill and I must go on Thursday."

I could have shaken her for her absurd reiteration of that obvious fiction, after she had told me her real reasons. She was determined to go, nor could our united entreaties move her in the least.

I did not tell Laura the legend of the shapes that walked in their marble, partly because a legend concerning our house might perhaps trouble my wife, and partly, I think, from some more occult reason. This was not quite the same to me as any other story, and I did not want to talk about it till the day was over. I had very soon ceased to think of the legend, however.

I was painting a portrait of Laura, against the lattice window, and I could not think of much else. I had got a splendid background of yellow and grey sunset, and was working away with enthusiasm at her lace.

On Thursday Mrs Dorman went. She relented, at parting, so far as to say, "Don't you put yourself about too much, ma'am, and if there's any little thing I can do next week, I'm sure I shan't mind." From which I inferred that she wished to come back to us after Halloween. Up to the last she adhered to the fiction of the niece with touching fidelity.

Thursday passed off pretty well. Laura showed marked

ability in the matter of steak and potatoes, and I confess that my knives, and the plates, which I insisted upon washing, were better done than I had dared to expect.

Friday came. It is about what happened on that Friday that this is written. I wonder if I should have believed it, if anyone had told it to me. I will write the story of it as quickly and plainly as I can. Everything that happened on that day is burnt into my brain. I shall not forget anything, nor leave anything out.

I got up early, I remember, and lighted the kitchen fire, and had just achieved a smoky success, when my little wife came running down, as sunny and sweet as the clear October morning itself. We prepared breakfast together, and found it very good fun. The housework was soon done, and when

brushes and brooms and pails were quiet again, the house was still indeed. It is wonderful what a difference one makes in a house. We really missed Mrs Dorman, quite apart from considerations concerning pots and pans. We spent the day in dusting our books and putting them straight, and dined gaily on cold steak and coffee.

Laura was, if possible, brighter and gayer and sweeter than usual, and I began to think that a little domestic toil was really good for her. We had never been so merry since we were married, and the walk we had that afternoon was, I think, the happiest time of all my life. When we had watched the deep scarlet clouds slowly pale into leaden grey against a pale-green sky, we came back to the house, silently, hand in hand.

"You are sad, my darling," I said, half-jestingly, as we sat down together in our little parlour. I expected a disclaimer, for my own silence had been the silence of complete happiness.

To my surprise she said, "Yes. I think I am sad, or rather I am uneasy. I don't think I'm very well. I have shivered three or four times since we came in, and it is not cold, is it?"

"No," I said, and hoped it was not a chill caught from the treacherous mists that roll up from the marshes in the dying light. No she said, she did not think so. Then, after a silence, she spoke suddenly,

"Do you ever have presentiments of evil?"

"No," I said, smiling, "and I shouldn't believe in them even if I had."

"I do," she went on; "the night my father died I knew it,

though he was right away in the north of Scotland." I did not answer in words.

She sat looking at the fire for some time in silence, gently stroking my hand. At last she sprang up, came behind me, and, drawing my head back, kissed me. "There, it's over now," she said. "What a baby I am! Come, light the candles, and we'll have some of these new Rubinstein duets."

And we spent a happy hour or two at the piano.

At about half past ten I began to long for the goodnight pipe, but Laura looked so white that I felt it would be brutal of me to fill our sitting-room with the fumes of strong cavendish. "I'll take my pipe outside," I said. "Let me come, too." "No, sweetheart, not tonight; you're much too tired. I shan't be long. Get to bed, or I shall have an invalid to nurse tomorrow as well as the boots to clean."

I kissed her and was turning to go, when she flung her arms round my neck, and held me as if she would never let me go again. I stroked her hair.

"Come darling, you're over-tired. The housework has been too much for you."

She loosened her clasp a little and drew a deep breath. "No. We've been very happy today, Jack, haven't we? Don't stay out too long."

"I won't, my dearie."

I strolled out of the front door, leaving it unlatched. What a night it was! The jagged masses of heavy dark cloud were rolling at intervals from horizon to horizon, and thin white wreaths covered the stars. Through all the rush of the cloud river, the moon swam, breasting the waves and disappearing again in the darkness. When now and again her light reached the woodlands they seemed to be slowly and noiselessly waving in time to the swing of the clouds above them. There was a strange grey light over all the earth; the fields had that shadowy bloom over them, which only comes from the marriage of dew and moonshine, or frost and starlight.

I walked up and down, drinking in the beauty of the quiet earth and the changing sky. The night was absolutely silent. Nothing seemed to be abroad. There was no skurrying of rabbits, or twitter of the half-asleep birds. And though the clouds went sailing across the sky, the wind that drove them never came low enough to rustle the dead leaves in the woodland paths. Across the meadows I could see the church tower standing out black and grey against the sky. I walked there thinking over our three months of happiness – and of my wife, her dear eyes, her loving ways. Oh, my little girl! My own little girl; what a vision came then of a long, glad life for you and me together!

I heard a bell-beat from the church. Eleven already! I turned to go in, but the night held me. I could not go back into our little warm rooms yet. I would go up to the church. I felt vaguely that it would be good to carry my love and thankfulness to the sanctuary whither so many loads of sorrow and gladness had been borne by the men and women of the dead years.

Man-Size in Marble

I looked in at the low window as I went by. Laura was half lying on her chair in front of the fire. I could not see her face; only her little head showed dark against the pale blue wall. She was quite still. Asleep, no doubt. My heart reached out to her, as I went on. There must be a God, I thought, and a God who was good. How otherwise could anything so sweet and dear as she have ever been imagined?

I walked slowly along the edge of the wood. A sound broke the stillness of the night; it was a rustling in the wood. I stopped and listened. The sound stopped too. I went on, and now distinctly heard another step than mine answer mine like an echo. It was a poacher or a wood-stealer, most likely, for these were not unknown in our Arcadian neighbourhood. But whoever it was, he was a fool not to step more lightly. I turned into the wood, and now the footstep seemed to come from the path I had just left. It must be an echo, I thought. The wood looked perfect in the moonlight. The large dying ferns and the brushwood showed where through thinning foliage the pale light came down. The tree trunks stood up like Gothic columns all around me. They reminded me of the church, and I turned into the bier-balk, and passed through the corpse-gate between the graves to the low porch. I paused for a moment on the stone seat where Laura and I had watched the fading landscape. Then I noticed that the door of the church was open, and I blamed myself for having left it unlatched the other night. We were the only people who ever cared to come to the church except on Sundays, and I was vexed to think that through our carelessness the damp autumn airs had had a chance of getting in and injuring the old fabric. I went in. It will seem strange, perhaps, that I should have gone halfway up the aisle before I remembered with a sudden chill, followed by as sudden a rush of self-contempt that this was the very day and hour when, according to tradition, the shapes drawed out man-size in marble began to walk.

Having thus remembered the legend, and remembered it with a shiver, of which I was ashamed, I could not do otherwise than walk up towards the altar, just to look at the figures as I said to myself; really what I wanted was to assure myself, first, that I did not believe the legend, and, secondly, that it was not true. I was rather glad that I had come. I thought now I could tell Mrs Dorman how vain her fancies were, and how peacefully the marble figures slept on through the ghastly hour. With my hands in my pockets I passed up the aisle. In the grey dim light the eastern end of the church looked larger than usual, and the arches above the two tombs looked larger too. The moon came out and showed me the reason. I stopped short, my heart gave a leap that nearly choked me, and then sank sickeningly.

The 'bodies drawed out man-size' *were gone,* and their marble slabs lay wide and bare in the vague moonlight that slanted through the east window.

Were they really gone? Or was I mad? Clenching my nerves, I stooped and passed my hand over the smooth slabs, and felt their flat unbroken surface. Had someone taken the things away? Was it some vile practical joke? I would make sure, anyway. In an instant I had made a torch of a newspaper, which happened to be in my pocket, and lighting it held it high above my head. Its yellow glare illumined the dark arches and those slabs. The figures *were* gone. And I was alone in the church; or was I alone?

And then a horror seized me, a horror indefinable and indescribable – an overwhelming certainty of supreme and accomplished calamity. I flung down the torch and tore along the aisle and out through the porch, biting my lips as I ran to keep myself from shrieking aloud. Oh, was I mad – or what was this that possessed me? I leapt the churchyard wall and took the straight cut across the fields, led by the light from our windows. Just as I got over the first stile, a dark figure seemed to spring out of the ground. Mad still with that certainty of misfortune, I made for the thing that stood in my path, shouting, "Get out of the way, can't you!"

But my push met with a more vigorous resistance than I had expected. My arms were caught just above the elbow and held as in a vice, and the raw-boned Irish doctor actually shook me.

"Would ye?" he cried, in his own unmistakable accents – "would ye, then?"

"Let me go, you fool," I gasped. "The marble figures have gone from the church; I tell you they've gone."

He broke into a ringing laugh. "I'll have to give ye a draught tomorrow, I see. Ye've listening to old wives' tales."

"I tell you, I've seen the bare slabs."

"Well, come back with me. I'm going up to old Palmer's –

his daughter's ill. We'll look in at the church and let me see the bare slabs."

"You go, if you like," I said, a little less frantic for his laughter. "I'm going home to my wife."

"Rubbish, man," said he. "D'ye think I'll permit of that? Are ye to go saying all yer life that ye've seen solid marble endowed with vitality, and me to go all me life saying ye were a coward? No, sir ye shan't do ut."

The night air, a human voice, and I think also the physical contact with this six feet of solid common sense, brought me back a little to my ordinary self, and the word 'coward' was a mental shower-bath.

"Come on, then," I said sullenly, "perhaps you're right."

He still held my arm tightly. We got over the stile and back to the church. All was still as death. The place smelt very damp and earthy. We walked up the aisle. I am not ashamed to confess that I shut my eyes: I knew the figures would not be there. I heard Kelly strike a match.

"Here they are, ye see, right enough; ye've been dreaming or drinking, asking yer pardon for the imputation."

I opened my eyes. By Kelly's expiring vesta I saw two shapes lying 'in their marble' on their slabs. I drew a deep breath, and caught his hand.

"I'm awfully indebted to you," I said. "It must have been some trick of light, or I have been working rather hard, perhaps that's it. Do you know, I was quite convinced they were gone."

"I'm aware of that," he answered, rather grimly, "ye'll have to be careful of that brain of yours, my friend, I assure ye."

He was leaning over and looking at the right-hand figure, whose stony face was the most villainous and deadly in expression.

"By Jove," he said, "something has been afoot here – this hand is broken."

And so it was. I was certain that it had been perfect the last time Laura and I had been there.

"Perhaps someone has tried to remove them," said the young doctor.

"That won't account for my impression," I objected.

"Too much painting and not enough rest will account for that, well enough."

"Come along," I said, "or my wife will be getting anxious. You'll come in and have a drop of whisky and drink confusion to ghosts and better sense to me."

"I ought to go up to Palmer's, but it's so late now I'd best leave it till the morning," he replied. "I was kept late at the Union, and I've had to see a lot of people since. All right, I'll come back with ye."

I think he fancied I needed him more than did Palmer's girl, so, discussing how such an illusion could have been possible, and deducing from this experience large generalities concerning ghostly apparitions, we walked up to our cottage. We saw, as we walked up the garden path, that bright light streamed out of the front door, and presently saw that the parlour door was open too. Had she gone out?

"Come in," I said, and Dr Kelly followed me into the parlour. It was ablaze with candles, not only the wax ones, but at least a dozen guttering, tallow dips, stuck in vases and ornaments in unlikely places. Light was Laura's remedy for nervousness. Poor child! Why had I left her? Brute that I was.

We glanced round the room, and at first we did not see her. The window was open, and the draught set all the candles flaring one way. Her chair was empty and her handkerchief and book lay on the floor. I turned to the window. There, in the recess of the window, I saw her. Oh, my child, my love, had she

gone to that window to watch for me? And what had come into the room behind her? To what had she turned with that look of frantic fear and horror? Oh, my little one, had she thought that it was I whose step she heard, and turned to meet what?

She had fallen back across a table in the window, and her body lay half on it and half on the window-seat, and her head hung down over the table, the brown hair loosened and fallen to the carpet. Her lips were drawn back, and her eyes wide open. They saw nothing now. What had they seen last?

The doctor moved towards her, but I pushed him aside and sprang to her; caught her in my arms and cried: "It's all right, Laura! I've got you safe darling." She fell into my arms in a heap. I clasped her and kissed her, and called her name, but I think I knew all the time that she was dead. Her hands were tightly clenched. In one of them she held something fast. When I was quite sure that she was dead, and that nothing mattered at all any more, I let him open her hand to see what she held.

It was a grey marble finger.

The Hound of the Baskervilles

Sir Arthur Conan Doyle

Extract

I have said that over the great Grimpen Mire there hung a dense, white fog. It was drifting slowly in our direction and banked itself up like a wall on that side of us, low but thick and well defined. The moon shone on it, and it looked like a great shimmering ice-field. Holmes' face was turned towards it, and he muttered impatiently as he watched its sluggish drift.

"It's moving towards us, Watson."

"Is that serious?"

"Very serious, indeed – the one thing upon earth which could have disarranged my plans. He can't be very long, now. It is already ten o'clock. Our success and even his life may depend upon his coming out before the fog is over the path."

The night was clear and fine. The stars shone cold and bright, while a half-moon bathed the whole scene in a soft, uncertain light. Before us lay the dark bulk of the house, its serrated roof and bristling chimneys hard outlined against the silver-spangled sky. Broad bars of golden light from the lower windows stretched across the orchard and the moor. One of them was suddenly shut off. There only remained the lamp in the dining room where the two men, the murderous host and the unconscious guest, still chatted over their cigars.

Every minute that white woolly plain that covered one-half of the moor was drifting closer and closer to the house. Already the first thin wisps of it were curling across the golden square of the lighted window. The farther wall of the orchard was already invisible, and the trees were standing out of a swirl of white vapour. As we watched it the fog-wreaths came crawling round both corners of the house and rolled slowly into one dense bank on which the upper floor and the roof floated like a strange ship upon a shadowy sea. Holmes struck his hand passionately upon the rock in front of us and stamped his feet in his impatience.

"If he isn't out in a quarter of an hour the path will be covered. In half an hour we won't be able to see our hands."

"Shall we move farther back upon higher ground?"

"Yes, I think it would be as well."

So as the fog-bank flowed onward we fell back before it until we were half a mile from the house, and still that dense white sea, with the moon silvering its upper edge, swept slowly and inexorably on. "We are going too far," said Holmes. "We dare not take the chance of his being overtaken before he can reach us. At all costs we must hold our ground where we are." He dropped on his knees and clapped his ear to the ground. "Thank God, I think that I hear him coming."

A sound of quick steps broke the silence of the moor. Crouching among the stones we stared intently at the silver-tipped bank in front of us. The steps grew louder, and through the fog, as through a curtain, there stepped the man whom we were awaiting. He looked round him in surprise as he emerged into the clear, starlit night. Then he came swiftly along the path, passed close to where we lay, and went on up the long slope behind us. As he walked he glanced continually over either shoulder, like a man who is ill at ease.

"Hist!" cried Holmes, and I heard the sharp click of a cocking pistol. "Look out! It's coming!"

There was a thin, crisp, continuous patter from somewhere in the heart of that crawling bank. The cloud was within fifty yards of where we lay, and we glared at it, all three, uncertain what horror was about to break from the heart of it. I was at holmes' elbow, and I glanced at his face. It was pale and exultant, his eyes shining brightly in the moonlight. But suddenly they started forward in a rigid, fixed stare, and his lips parted in amazement. At the same instant Lestrade gave a yell of terror and threw himself face downward upon the ground. I sprang to my feet, my inert hand grasping my pistol, my mind

paralyzed by the dreadful shape that had sprung out upon us from the shadows of the fog. A hound it was, an enormous coal-black hound, but not such a hound as mortal eyes have ever seen. Fire burst from its open mouth, its eyes glowed with a smouldering glare, its muzzle and hackles and dewlap were outlined in flickering flame. Never could anything more savage, more hellish be conceived than that dark form and savage face which broke upon us out of the wall of fog.

With long bounds the huge black creature was leaping down the track, following hard upon the footsteps of our friend. So paralyzed were we by the apparition that we allowed him to pass before we had recovered our nerve. Then Holmes and I both fired together, and the creature gave a hideous howl, which showed that one at least had hit him. He did not pause, however, but bounded onwards. Far away on the path we saw Sir Henry looking back, his face white in the moonlight, his hands raised in horror, glaring helplessly at the frightful thing.

But that cry of pain from the hound had blown all our fears to the winds. If he was vulnerable he was mortal, and if we could wound him we could kill him. Never have I seen a man run as Holmes ran that night. I am reckoned fleet of foot, but he outpaced me as much as I outpaced the little professional. In front of us as we flew up the track we heard scream after scream from Sir Henry and the deep roar of the hound. I was in time to see the beast spring upon its victim, hurl him to the ground, and worry at his throat. But the next instant Holmes had emptied five barrels of his revolver into the creature's flank. With a last howl of agony and a vicious snap in the air, it rolled upon its back, four feet pawing furiously, and then fell limp upon its side. The giant hound was dead.

Sir Henry lay insensible where he had fallen. We tore away his collar, and Holmes breathed a prayer of gratitude when we saw that there was no sign of a wound and that the rescue had been in time. Already our friend's eyelids shivered. Lestrade thrust his brandy flask between the baronet's teeth, and two frightened eyes were looking up at us.

"My God!" he whispered. "Whatever, was it?"

"It's dead, whatever it is," said Holmes. "We've laid the family ghost once and forever."

Some Words With a Mummy

Edgar Allan Poe
Extract

I could not have completed my third snore when there came a furious ringing at the doorbell, and then an impatient thumping at the knocker, which awakened me at once. In a minute afterward, and while I was still rubbing my eyes, my wife thrust in my face a note, from my old friend, Dr Ponnonner. It ran thus:

Come to me, by all means, my dear good friend, as soon as you receive this. Come and help us to rejoice. At last, by long persevering diplomacy, I have gained the assent of the

240

Some Words with a Mummy

Directors of the City Museum, to my examination of the mummy – you know the one I mean. I have permission to unswathe it and open it, if desirable. A few friends only will be present – you, of course. The mummy is now at my house, and we shall begin to unroll it at eleven tonight.

Yours, ever, Ponnonncr.

By the time I had reached the Ponnonner, it struck me that I was as wide awake as a man need be. I leapt out of bed in an ecstacy, overthrowing all in my way; dressed myself with a rapidity truly marvellous; and set off, at the top of my speed, for the doctor's.

There I found a very eager company assembled. They had been awaiting me with much impatience; the mummy was extended upon the dining table; and the moment I entered its examination was commenced.

It was one of a pair brought, several years previously, by Captain Arthur Sabretash, a cousin of Ponnonner's from a tomb near Eleithias, in the Lybian mountains, a considerable distance above Thebes on the Nile. The grottoes at this point, although less magnificent than the Theban sepulchres, are of higher interest, on account of affording more numerous illustrations of the private life of the Egyptians. The chamber from which our specimen was taken, was said to be very rich in such illustrations; the walls being completely covered with fresco paintings and bas-reliefs, while statues, vases, and mosaic work of rich patterns, indicated the vast wealth of the deceased.

The treasure had been deposited in the Museum precisely in the same condition in which Captain Sabretash had found it – that is to say, the coffin had not been disturbed. For eight years it had thus stood, subject only externally to public inspection. We had now, therefore, the complete mummy at our disposal; and to those who are aware how very rarely the unransacked antique reaches our shores, it will be evident, at once, that we had great reason to congratulate ourselves upon our good fortune.

Approaching the table, I saw on it a large box, or case, nearly seven feet long, and perhaps three feet wide, by two feet and a half deep. It was oblong – not coffin-shaped. The material was at first supposed to be the wood of the sycamore (*platanus*), but, upon cutting into it, we found it to be pasteboard, or, more properly, pâpier-maché, composed of papyrus. It was thickly ornamented with paintings, representing funeral scenes, and other mournful subjects – interspersed among which, in every variety of position, were certain series of hieroglyphical characters, intended, no doubt, for the name of the departed. By good luck Mr Gliddon formed one of our party, and he had no difficulty in translating the letters, which were simply phonetic, and represented the word, *Allamistakeo*.

We had some difficulty in getting this case open without injury; but having at length accomplished the task, we came to a second, coffin-shaped, and very considerably less in size than the exterior one, but resembling it precisely in every other respect. The interval between the two was filled with resin, which had, in some degree, defaced the colours of the interior box.

Upon opening this latter (which we did quite easily), we arrived at a third case, also coffin-shaped, and varying from the second one in no particular, except in that of its material, which was cedar, and still emitted the peculiar and highly aromatic odour of that wood. Between the second and the third case there was no interval – the one fitting accurately within the other.

Removing the third case, we discovered and took out the body itself. We had expected to find it, as usual, enveloped in frequent rolls or bandages, of linen; but, in place of these, we found a sort of sheath, made of papyrus, and coated with a layer of plaster, thickly gilt and painted. The paintings represented subjects connected with the various supposed duties of the soul, and its presentation to different divinities, with numerous identical human figures intended, very probably, as portraits of the persons embalmed. Extending from head to foot was a columnar, or perpendicular, inscription, in phonetic hieroglyphics, giving again his name and titles, and the names and titles of his relations.

Around the neck thus ensheathed, was a collar of cylindrical glass beads, diverse in colour, and so arranged as to form images of deities, of the scarabaeus, etc. with the winged globe. Around the small of the waist was a similar collar or belt.

Stripping off the papyrus, we found the flesh in excellent preservation, with no perceptible odour. The colour was reddish. The skin was hard, smooth, and glossy. The teeth and hair were in good condition. The eyes (it seemed) had been removed, and glass ones substituted, which were very beautiful and wonderfully lifelike, with the exception of somewhat too determined a stare. The fingers and the nails were brilliantly gilded.

Mr Gliddon was of opinion, from the redness of the epidermis, that the embalmment had been effected altogether by asphaltum; but, on scraping the surface with a steel instrument, and throwing into the fire some of the powder thus obtained, the flavour of camphor and other sweet-scented gums became apparent.

We searched the corpse very carefully for the usual openings through which the entrails are extracted, but, to our surprise, we could discover none. No member of the party was at that period aware that entire or unopened mummies are not infrequently met. The brain it was customary to withdraw through the nose; the intestines through an incision in the side. The body was then shaved, washed, and salted; then laid aside for several weeks, when the operation of embalming, properly so called, began.

As no trace of an opening could be found, Dr Ponnonner was preparing his instruments for dissection, when I observed that it was then past two o'clock. Hereupon it was agreed to postpone the internal examination until the next evening; and we were about to separate for the present, when someone suggested an experiment or two with the Voltaic pile.

Some Words With a Mummy

The application of electricity to a mummy that was at least three or four thousand years old, was an idea, if not particularly sage, still sufficiently original, and we all caught it at once. About one-tenth in earnest and nine-tenths in jest, we arranged a battery in the doctor's study, and conveyed thither the Egyptian.

It was only after much trouble that we succeeded in laying bare some portions of the temporal muscle which appeared of less stony rigidity than other parts of the frame, but which, as we had anticipated, of course, gave no indication of galvanic susceptibility when brought in contact with the wire. This, the first trial, indeed, seemed decisive, and, with a hearty laugh at our own absurdity, we were bidding each other goodnight, when my eyes, happening to fall upon those of the mummy, were there immediately riveted in amazement. My brief glance, in fact, had sufficed to assure me that the orbs which we had all supposed to be glass, and which were originally very noticeable for a certain wild stare, were now so far covered by the lids, that only a small portion of the *tunica albuginea* remained visible.

With a shout I called attention to the fact, and it became immediately obvious to all.

I cannot say that I was *alarmed* at the phenomenon, because alarmed is, in my case, not exactly the word. It is possible, however, that, but for the brown stout, I might have been a little nervous. As for the rest of the company, they really made no attempt at concealing the downright fright which possessed them. Dr Ponnonner was a man to be pitied. Mr Gliddon, by some peculiar process, managed to render himself invisible. Mr Silk Buckingham, I fancy, will scarcely be so bold as to deny the fact that he immediately made his way, upon all fours, under the table.

After the first shock of astonishment, however, we resolved, as a matter of course, upon further experiment forthwith. Our operations were now directed against the great toe of the right foot. We made an incision over the outside of the exterior *os sesamoideum pollicis pedis,* and thus got at the root of the *abductor* muscle. Readjusting the battery, we now applied the fluid to the bisected nerves – when, with a movement of exceeding life-likeness, the mummy first drew up its right knee so as to bring it nearly in contact with the abdomen, and then, straightening the limb with inconceivable force, bestowed a kick upon Dr Ponnonner, which had the effect of discharging that gentleman, like an arrow from a catapult, through a window into the street below.

We rushed out *en masse* to bring in the mangled remains of the victim, but had the happiness to meet him upon the staircase, coming up in an unaccountable hurry, brimful of the most ardent philosophy, and impressed with the necessity of prosecuting our experiment with vigour and with zeal.

It was by his advice, accordingly, that we made, upon the spot, a profound incision into the tip of the subject's nose, while the doctor himself, laying violent hands upon it, pulled it into vehement contact with the wire.

Some Words With a Mummy

Morally and physically – figuratively and literally – was the effect electric. In the first place, the corpse opened its eyes and winked very rapidly for several minutes, as does Mr Barnes in the pantomime, in the second place, it sneezed and in the third it sat up on end...

carmilla

J Sheridan Le Fanu

Extract

The general was still agitated. "She called herself Carmilla?" he asked.

"Carmilla, yes," I answered.

"Aye," he said; "that is Millarca. That is the same person who long ago was called many other names – Mircalla, Countess Karnstein. Depart from this accursed ground, my poor child, as quickly as you can. Drive to the clergyman's house, and stay there till we come. Only there will you be safe."

As he spoke, one of the strangest-looking men I ever beheld entered the chapel. He was tall, narrow-chested, stooping, with high shoulders, and dressed in black. His face was brown and dried in with deep furrows and he wore an oddly-shaped hat with a broad leaf. His hair, long and grizzled, hung on his shoulders. He wore a pair of gold spectacles, and walked slowly with an odd shambling gait, with his face sometimes turned up to the sky and sometimes bowed down towards the ground, seemed to wear a perpetual smile. His long thin arms were swinging, and his lank hands, in old black gloves ever so much too wide for them, waving and gesticulating in utter abstraction.

"The very man!" exclaimed the general, advancing with manifest delight. "My dear baron, how happy I am to see you, I had no hope of meeting you so soon." He signed to my father, who had by this time returned, and leading the fantastic old gentleman, whom he called the baron, to meet him, he introduced him formally, and they at once entered into earnest conversation. The stranger took a roll of paper from his pocket, and spread it on the worn surface of a tomb that stood by. He had a pencil case in his fingers, with which he traced imaginary lines from point to point on the paper, which from their often glancing from it together at certain points of the building, I concluded to be a plan of the chapel. He accompanied what I may term his lecture, with occasional readings from a dirty little book, whose yellow leaves were closely written over.

They sauntered together down the side aisle, opposite to the spot where I was standing, conversing as they went. Then they began measuring distances by paces, and finally they all stood together, facing a piece of the sidewall, which they began to examine with great minuteness; pulling off the ivy that clung over it, and rapping the plaster with the ends of their sticks. At length they ascertained the existence of a broad marble tablet, with letters carved in relief upon it.

With the assistance of the woodman, who soon returned, a monumental inscription, and carved coat-of-arms, were disclosed. They proved to be those of the long-lost monument of Mircalla, Countess Karnstein.

The old general, though not I fear given to the praying mood, raised his hands and eyes to heaven, in mute thanksgiving for some moments.

"Tomorrow," I heard him say; "the commissioner will be here, and the inquisition will be held according to law."

Then turning to the old man with the gold spectacles, whom I have described, he shook him warmly by both hands and said: "How can I thank you? How can we all thank you? You will have delivered this region from a plague that has scourged its inhabitants for more than a century."

My father led the stranger aside, and the general followed. I knew that he had led them out of hearing, that he might relate my case, and I saw them glance often quickly at me, as the discussion proceeded.

My father came to me, kissed me again and again, and leading me from the chapel, said: "It is time to return, but before we go home, we must add to our party the good priest, who lives but a little way from this; and persuade him to accompany us to the *schloss*."

In this quest we were successful: and I was glad, being unspeakably fatigued when we reached home. But my satisfaction was changed to dismay, on discovering that there were no tidings of Carmilla. The arrangements for the night were singular. Two servants, and *madame* were to sit up in my room that night; and the ecclesiastic with my father kept watch in the adjoining dressing room.

The priest had performed certain solemn rites that night, the purport of which I did not understand any more than I comprehended the reason of this extraordinary precaution taken for my safety during sleep.

I saw all clearly a few days later.

The disappearance of Carmilla was followed by the discontinuance of my nightly sufferings.

You have heard, no doubt, of the appalling superstition that prevails in Upper and Lower Styria, in Moravia, Silesia, in Turkish Servia, in Poland, even in Russia; the superstition, so we must call it, of the vampire.

If human testimony – taken with every care and solemnity, judicially, before commissions innumerable, each consisting of many members all chosen for integrity and intelligence, and constituting reports more voluminous perhaps than exist upon any one other class of cases – is worth anything, it is difficult to deny, or even to doubt the existence of such a phenomenon as the vampire.

For my part I have heard no theory by which to explain what I myself have witnessed and experienced, other than that supplied by the ancient and well-attested belief of the country.

The next day the formal proceedings took place in the Chapel of Karnstein. The grave of the Countess Mircalla was

opened; and the general and my father recognized each his perfidious and beautiful guest, in the face now disclosed to view. The features, though a hundred and fifty years had passed since her funeral, were tinted with the warmth of life. The two medical men attested the marvellous fact that there was a faint but appreciable respiration, and a corresponding action of the heart. The limbs were perfectly flexible, the flesh elastic; and the leaden coffin floated with blood. Here then, were all the admitted signs and proofs of vampirism. The body therefore, in accordance with the ancient practice, was raised and a sharp stake driven through the heart of the vampire, who uttered a piercing shriek at the moment, in all respects such as might escape from a living person in the last agony. Then the head was struck off, and a torrent of blood flowed from the severed neck. The body and head was next placed on a pile of wood, and reduced to ashes, which were thrown upon the river and borne away, and that territory has never since been plagued by the visits of a vampire.

My father has a copy of the report of the Imperial Commission, with the signatures of all who were present at these proceedings, attached in verification of the statement. It is from this official paper that I have summarized my account of this last shocking scene.

Notes on the Authors

Find out more about some of the authors featured in this book.

Emily Brontë (1818–1848)

The classic tale *Wuthering Heights* (1847) was set on the wild Yorkshire moors around the author's lonely home. She was the daughter of a parson, but her passionate, haunting tragedy tells of an afterlife disturbingly different from Christian beliefs.

Sir Arthur Conan Doyle (1859–1930)

A doctor, keen spiritualist, and writer best-known for his Sherlock Holmes detective thrillers, Conan Doyle rooted *The Hound of the Baskervilles* in British folklore. When the story was first published in *The Strand* (1901), the magazine went into seven printings for the only time in its history.

Joseph Sheridan Le Fanu (1814–1873)

As a young man, Le Fanu started writing supernatural stories. After the death of his wife in his mid-forties, he became a recluse and devoted himself entirely to composing uncanny tales. He was a bestselling author in his day for works such as the vampire novel *Carmilla* (1871–1872) and a short story collection *In a Glass Darkly* (1872).

Mary Shelley (1797–1851)

In 1816 Shelley went on holiday to Switzerland with the poets Percy Bysshe Shelley (her husband) and Lord Byron (their friend). Bad weather kept them indoors and they entertained themselves by reading ghost stories aloud. Byron challenged them to write their own, and Shelley – then just nineteen – created the gothic horror classic, *Frankenstein*.

Bram Stoker (1847–1912)

Born and educated in Dublin, Stoker was manager of London's Lyceum Theatre. A pillar of respectable Victorian society, he spent his spare moments writing supernatural short stories and novels, including the bestseller *Dracula* (1897).

Oscar Wilde (1854–1900)

An Irish writer whose body of work includes poetry, plays and short stories, Wilde wrote just one novel: *The Picture of Dorian Gray*. This supernatural tale so unsettled and shocked readers that it caused a scandal when it was first printed in *Lippincott's Magazine* in 1890.

First published by Bardfield Press in 2007
Copyright © Miles Kelly Publishing Ltd 2007

Bardfield Press is an imprint of Miles Kelly Publishing Ltd
Bardfield Centre, Great Bardfield, Essex, CM7 4SL

Some of this material appears in *Ghost Stories*

2 4 6 8 10 9 7 5 3 1

Editorial Director Belinda Gallagher
Art Director Jo Brewer
Assistant Editors Rosalind McGuire, Hannah Todd
Designer Tom Slemmings
Picture Researcher Laura Faulder
Production Elizabeth Brunwin
Reprographics Anthony Cambray, Stephan Davis,
Liberty Newton, Ian Paulyn

British Library Cataloguing-in-Publication Data
A catalogue record for this book is available from the British Library

ISBN 978-1-84236-775-9

Printed in China

All artworks are from the Miles Kelly Artwork Bank

All photographs from:
Castrol CMCD Corbis Corel digitalSTOCK digitalvision
Flat Earth Hemera ILN John Foxx PhotoAlto PhotoDisc
PhotoEssentials PhotoPro Stockbyte

www.mileskelly.net
info@mileskelly.net